S.F.   Clarke, Arthur C

The songs of
distant earth

DATE DUE

S.F.   Clarke, Arthur C

The songs of
distant earth

DATE	ISSUED TO
SEP 1 9 1986	86-194
OCT 3 1986	86-194 renewed
OCT 1 7 1986	86-194 renewed
NOV 3 1986	81-381

THE SONGS OF DISTANT EARTH

BOOKS BY ARTHUR C. CLARKE

Non-Fiction

Ascent to Orbit
Boy Beneath the Sea
The Challenge of the Sea
The Challenge of the Spaceship
The Coast of Coral
The Exploration of the Moon
The Exploration of Space
The First Five Fathoms
Going into Space
Indian Ocean Adventure
Indian Ocean Treasure
Interplanetary Flight
The Making of a Moon
Profiles of the Future
The Promise of Space
The Reefs of Taprobane
Report on Planet Three
The Treasure of the Great Reef
The View from Serendip
Voice Across the Sea
Voices from the Sky
1984: Spring—A Choice of Futures

With the Editors of "LIFE"
Man and Space

With the Astronauts
First on the Moon

With Robert Silverberg
Into Space

With Chesley Bonestell
Beyond Jupiter

With Simon Welfare &
John Fairley
Arthur C. Clarke's
Mysterious World
Arthur C. Clarke's
World of Strange Powers

With Peter Hyams
The Odyssey File

Fiction

*Across the Sea of Stars
Against the Fall of Night
Childhood's End
The City and the Stars
The Deep Range
Dolphin Island
Earthlight
*Expedition to Earth
A Fall of Moondust
The Fountains of Paradise
*From the Oceans, from the Stars
Glide Path
Imperial Earth
Islands in the Sky
The Lion of Comarre
The Lost Worlds of 2001
*The Nine Billion Names of God
*The Other Side of the Sky
*Prelude to Mars
Prelude to Space
Reach for Tomorrow
Rendezvous with Rama
The Sands of Mars
*The Sentinel
*Tales from the "White Hart"
*Tales of Ten Worlds
The Wind from the Sun
2010: Odyssey Two

With Stanley Kubrick
2001: A Space Odyssey

*Anthologies

Arthur Clarke has also edited:

The Coming of the Space Age

Science Fiction Hall of Fame, III
Three for Tomorrow
Time Probe

ARTHUR C. CLARKE

THE SONGS OF DISTANT EARTH

 A DEL REY BOOK   BALLANTINE BOOKS   NEW YORK

Library of Congress Cataloging-in-Publication Data

Clarke, Arthur Charles, 1917–
    The songs of distant earth.
    "A Del Rey book"
    I. Title.
PR6005.L36S66 1986   823'.914   85–26825
ISBN 0–345–33219–9
ISBN 0–345–33525–2 (Limited Edition)

Manufactured in the United States of America

Design by Holly Johnson

10 9 8 7 6 5 4 3 2

S. F.

For Tamara and Cherene,
Valerie and Hector
—for love and loyalty

CONTENTS

V. THE *BOUNTY* SYNDROME

VI. THE FORESTS OF THE SEA

VII. AS THE SPARKS FLY UPWARD

VIII. THE SONGS OF DISTANT EARTH

IX. SAGAN TWO

Nowhere in all space or on a thousand worlds will there be men to share our loneliness. There may be wisdom; there may be power; somewhere across space great instruments . . . may stare vainly at our floating cloud wrack, their owners yearning as we yearn. Nevertheless, in the nature of life and in the principles of evolution we have had our answer. Of men elsewhere, and beyond, there will be none forever . . .

Loren Eiseley,
The Immense Journey (1957)

I have written a wicked book, and feel spotless as the lamb.

Melville to Hawthorne (1851)

AUTHOR'S NOTE

This novel is based on an idea developed almost thirty years ago in a short story of the same name (now in my collection *The Other Side of the Sky*). However, this version was directly—and *negatively*—inspired by the recent rash of space-operas on TV and movie screen. (Query: what is the opposite of inspiration—expiration?)

Please do not misunderstand me: I have enormously enjoyed the best of *Star Trek* and the Lucas/Spielberg epics, to mention only the most famous examples of the *genre*. But these works are fantasy, not science fiction in the strict meaning of the term. It now seems almost certain that in the real universe we may never exceed the velocity of light. Even the very closest star systems will always be decades or centuries apart; no Warp Six will ever get you from one episode to another in time for next week's installment. The great Producer in the Sky did not arrange his program planning that way.

In the last decade, there has also been a significant, and rather surprising, change in the attitude of scientists toward the problem of Extraterrestrial Intelligence. The whole subject did not become respectable (except among dubious characters like the writers of science fiction) until the 1960s: Shklovskii and Sagan's *Intelligent Life in the Universe* (1966) is the landmark here.

But now there has been a backlash. The total failure to find any trace of life in this Solar System, or to pick up any of the interstellar radio signals that our great antennas should be easily able to detect, has prompted some scientists to argue "Perhaps we *are* alone in the Universe. . ." Dr Frank Tipler, the best-known exponent of this view, has (doubtless deliberately) outraged the Saganites by giving one of his papers the provocative title "There Are No Intelligent Extra-Terrestrials." Carl Sagan *et al* argue (and I agree with them) that it is much too early to jump to such far-reaching conclusions.

Meanwhile, the controversy rages; as has been well said, *either* answer will be awe-inspiring. The question can only be settled by evidence, not by any amount of logic, however plausible. I would like to see the whole debate given a decade or two of benign neglect, while the radioastronomers, like gold miners panning for dust, quietly sieve through the torrents of noise pouring down from the sky.

This novel is, among other things, my attempt to create a wholly *realistic* piece of fiction on the interstellar theme—just as, in *Prelude to Space* (1951), I used known or foreseeable technology to depict mankind's first voyage beyond the Earth. There is nothing in this book that defies or denies known principles; the only really wild extrapolation is the "quantum drive," and even this has a highly respectable paternity. (See Acknowledgments.) Should it turn out to be a pipe-dream, there are several possible alternatives; and if we twentieth-century primitives can imagine them, future science will undoubtedly discover something much better.

Arthur C. Clarke
Colombo, Sri Lanka, July 3, 1985

I. THALASSA

1. THE BEACH AT TARNA

Even before the boat came through the reef, Mirissa could tell that Brant was angry. The tense attitude of his body as he stood at the wheel—the very fact that he had not left the final passage in Kumar's capable hands—showed that something had upset him.

She left the shade of the palm trees and walked slowly down the beach, the wet sand tugging at her feet. When she reached the water's edge, Kumar was already furling the sail. Her "baby" brother—now almost as tall as she was, and solid muscle—waved to her cheerfully. How often she had wished that Brant shared Kumar's easygoing good nature, which no crisis ever seemed capable of disturbing . . .

Brant did not wait for the boat to hit the sand, but jumped into the water while it was still waist deep and came splashing angrily toward her. He was carrying a twisted mass of metal festooned with broken wires and held it up for her inspection.

"Look!" he cried. "They've done it again!"

With his free hand, he waved toward the northern horizon.

"This time—I'm not going to let them get away with it! And the mayor can say what she damn well pleases!"

Mirissa stood aside while the little catamaran, like some primeval sea-beast making its first assault on the dry land, heaved itself slowly up the beach on its spinning outboard rollers. As soon as it was above the high-water line, Kumar stopped the engine and jumped out to join his still-fuming skipper.

"I keep telling Brant," he said, "that it must be an acci-

3

dent—maybe a dragging anchor. After all, why should the Northers do something like this *deliberately*?

"I'll tell you," Brant retorted. "Because they're too lazy to work out the technology themselves. Because they're afraid we'll catch too many fish. Because—"

He caught sight of the other's grin and sent the cat's cradle of broken wires spinning in his direction. Kumar caught it effortlessly.

"Anyway—even if it *is* an accident, they shouldn't be anchoring here. That area's clearly marked on the chart: KEEP OUT—RESEARCH PROJECT. So I'm still going to lodge a protest."

Brant had already recovered his good humor; even his most furious rages seldom lasted more than a few minutes. To keep him in the right mood, Mirissa started to run her fingers down his back and spoke to him in her most soothing voice.

"Did you catch any good fish?"

"Of course not," Kumar answered. "He's only interested in catching statistics—kilograms per kilowatt—that sort of nonsense. Lucky I took my rod. We'll have tuna for dinner."

He reached into the boat and pulled out almost a meter of streamlined power and beauty, its colors fading rapidly, its sightless eyes already glazed in death.

"Don't often get one of these," he said proudly. They were still admiring his prize when History returned to Thalassa, and the simple, carefree world they had known all their young lives came abruptly to its end.

The sign of its passing was written there upon the sky as if a giant hand had drawn a piece of chalk across the blue dome of heaven. Even as they watched, the gleaming vapor trail began to fray at the edges, breaking up into wisps of cloud, until it seemed that a bridge of snow had been thrown from horizon to horizon.

And now a distant thunder was rolling down from the edge of space. It was a sound that Thalassa had not heard for seven hundred years but which any child would recognize at once.

Despite the warmth of the evening, Mirissa shivered and

4

her hand found Brant's. Though his fingers closed about hers, he scarcely seemed to notice; he was still staring at the riven sky.

Even Kumar was subdued, yet he was the first to speak. "One of the colonies must have found us."

Brant shook his head slowly but without much conviction. "Why should they bother? They must have the old maps—they'll know that Thalassa is almost all ocean. It wouldn't make any sense to come here."

"Scientific curiosity?" Mirissa suggested. "To see what's happened to us? I always said we should repair the communications link . . ."

This was an old dispute, which was revived every few decades. One day, most people agreed, Thalassa really should rebuild the big dish on East Island, destroyed when Krakan erupted four hundred years ago. But meanwhile there was so much that was more important—or simply more amusing.

"Building a starship's an *enormous* project," Brant said thoughtfully. "I don't believe that any colony would do it—unless it had to. Like Earth . . ."

His voice trailed off into silence. After all these centuries, that was still a hard name to say.

As one person, they turned toward the east, where the swift equatorial night was advancing across the sea.

A few of the brighter stars had already emerged, and just climbing above the palm trees was the unmistakable, compact little group of the Triangle. Its three stars were of almost equal magnitude—but a far more brilliant intruder had once shone, for a few weeks, near the southern tip of the constellation.

Its now-shrunken husk was still visible, in a telescope of moderate power. But no instrument could show the orbiting cinder that had been the planet Earth.

2. THE LITTLE NEUTRAL ONE

More than a thousand years later, a great historian had called the period 1901–2000 "the Century when everything happened." He added that the people of the time would have agreed with him—but for entirely the wrong reasons.

They would have pointed, often with justified pride, to the era's scientific achievements—the conquest of the air, the release of atomic energy, the discovery of the basic principles of life, the electronics and communications revolution, the beginnings of artificial intelligence, and most spectacular of all, the exploration of the solar system and the first landing on the Moon. But as the historian pointed out, with the 20/20 accuracy of hindsight, not one in a thousand would even have heard of the discovery that transcended all these events by threatening to make them utterly irrelevant.

It seemed as harmless, and as far from human affairs, as the fogged photographic plate in Becquerel's laboratory that led, in only fifty years, to the fireball above Hiroshima. Indeed, it was a by-product of that same research and began in equal innocence.

Nature is a very strict accountant and always balances her books. So physicists were extremely puzzled when they discovered certain nuclear reactions in which, after all the fragments were added up, something seemed to be missing on one side of the equation.

Like a bookkeeper hastily replenishing the petty cash to keep one jump ahead of the auditors, the physicists were forced to invent a new particle. And, to account for the discrepancy, it had to be a most peculiar one—with neither mass nor charge, and so fantastically penetrating that it could pass, without noticeable inconvenience, through a wall of lead *billions* of kilometers thick.

This phantom was given the nickname "neutrino"—neutron plus bambino. There seemed no hope of ever detecting so elusive an entity; but in 1956, by heroic feats of instrumentation, the physicists had caught the first few specimens. It was also a triumph for the theoreticians, who now found their unlikely equations verified.

The world as a whole neither knew nor cared; but the countdown to doomsday had begun.

3. VILLAGE COUNCIL

Tarna's local network was never more than ninety-five percent operational—but on the other hand never *less* than eighty-five percent of it was working at any one time. Like most of the equipment on Thalassa, it had been designed by long-dead geniuses so that catastrophic breakdowns were virtually impossible. Even if many components failed, the system would still continue to function reasonably well until someone was sufficiently exasperated to make repairs.

The engineers called this "graceful degradation"—a phrase that, some cynics had declared, rather accurately described the Lassan way of life.

According to the central computer, the network was now hovering around its normal ninety percent serviceability, and Mayor Waldron would gladly have settled for less. Most of the village had called her during the past half hour, and at least fifty adults and children were milling round in the council chamber—which was more than it could comfortably hold, let alone seat. The quorum for an ordinary meeting was twelve, and it sometimes took draconian measures to collect even that number of warm bodies in one place. The rest of Tarna's five hundred and sixty inhabitants preferred to watch—and vote, if they felt sufficiently interested—in the comfort of their own homes.

There had also been two calls from the provincial governor, one from the president's office, and one from the North Island news service, all making the same completely unnecessary request. Each had received the same short answer: Of course

8

we'll tell you if anything happens . . . and thanks for your interest.

Mayor Waldron did not like excitement, and her moderately successful career as a local administrator had been based on avoiding it. Sometimes, of course, that was impossible; her veto would hardly have deflected the hurricane of '09, which—until today—had been the century's most notable event.

"Quiet, everybody!" she cried. "Reena—leave those shells alone—someone went to a lot of trouble arranging them! Time you were in bed, anyway! Billy—off the table! *Now!*"

The surprising speed with which order was restored showed that, for once, the villagers were anxious to hear what their mayor had to say. She switched off the insistent beeping of her wrist-phone and routed the call to the message center.

"Frankly, I don't know much more than you do—and it's not likely we'll get any more information for several hours. But it certainly *was* some kind of spacecraft, and it had already reentered—I suppose I should say entered—when it passed over us. Since there's nowhere else for it to go on Thalassa, presumably it will come back to the Three Islands sooner or later. That might take hours if it's going right round the planet."

"Any attempt at radio contact?" somebody asked.

"Yes, but no luck so far."

"Should we even try?" an anxious voice said.

A brief hush fell upon the whole assembly; then Councillor Simmons, Mayor Waldron's chief gadfly, gave a snort of disgust.

"That's ridiculous. Whatever we do, they can find us in about ten minutes. Anyway, they probably know exactly where we are."

"I agree completely with the councillor," Mayor Waldron said, relishing this unusual opportunity. "Any colony ship

9

will certainly have maps of Thalassa. They may be a thousand years old—but they'll show First Landing."

"But suppose—just suppose—that they *are* aliens?"

The mayor sighed; she thought that thesis had died through sheer exhaustion centuries ago.

"There are no aliens," she said firmly. "At least none intelligent enough to go starfaring. Of course, we can never be one hundred percent certain—but Earth searched for a thousand years with every conceivable instrument."

"There's another possibility," said Mirissa, who was standing with Brant and Kumar near the back of the chamber. Every head turned toward her, but Brant looked slightly annoyed. Despite his love for Mirissa, there were times when he wished that she was not quite so well informed and that her family had not been in charge of the Archives for the last five generations.

"What's that, my dear?"

Now it was Mirissa's turn to be annoyed, though she concealed her irritation. She did not enjoy being condescended to by someone who was not really very intelligent, though undoubtedly shrewd—or perhaps cunning was the better word. The fact that Mayor Waldron was always making eyes at Brant did not bother Mirissa in the least; it merely amused her, and she could even feel a certain sympathy for the older woman.

"It could be another robot seedship, like the one that brought our ancestor's gene patterns to Thalassa."

"But *now*—so late?"

"Why not? The first seeders could only reach a few percent of light velocity. Earth kept improving them—right up to the time it was destroyed. As the later models were almost ten times faster, the earlier ones were overtaken in a century or so; many of them must still be on the way. Don't you agree, Brant?"

Mirissa was always careful to bring him into any discussion and, if possible, to make him think he had originated it. She was well aware of his feelings of inferiority and did not wish to add to them.

Sometimes it was rather lonely being the brightest person in Tarna; although she networked with half a dozen of her mental peers on the Three Islands, she seldom met them in the face-to-face encounters that, even after all these millennia, no communications technology could really match.

"It's an interesting idea," Brant said. "You could be right."

Although history was not his strong point, Brant Falconer had a technician's knowledge of the complex series of events that had led to the colonization of Thalassa. "And what shall we do," he asked, "if it's another seedship, and tries to colonize us all over again? Say, 'Thanks very much, but not today'?"

There were a few nervous little laughs; then Councillor Simmons remarked thoughtfully, "I'm sure we could handle a seedship if we had to. And wouldn't its robots be intelligent enough to cancel their program when they saw that the job had already been done?"

"Perhaps. But they might think they could do a better one. Anyway, whether it's a relic from Earth or a later model from one of the colonies, it's bound to be a robot of some kind."

There was no need to elaborate; everyone knew the fantastic difficulty and expense of *manned* interstellar flight. Even though technically possible, it was completely pointless. Robots could do the job a thousand times more cheaply.

"Robot or relic—what are we going to do about it?" one of the villagers demanded.

"It may not be our problem," the mayor said. "Everyone seems to have assumed that it will head for First Landing, but why should it? After all, North Island is much more likely—"

The mayor had often been proved wrong, but never so swiftly. This time the sound that grew in the sky above Tarna was no distant thunder from the ionosphere but the piercing whistle of a low, fast-flying jet. Everyone rushed out of the council chamber in unseemly haste; only the first few were in

11

time to see the blunt-nosed delta-wing eclipsing the stars as it headed purposefully toward the spot still sacred as the last link with Earth.

Mayor Waldron paused briefly to report to central, then joined the others milling around outside.

"Brant—you can get there first. Take the kite."

Tarna's chief mechanical engineer blinked; it was the first time he had ever received so direct an order from the mayor. Then he looked a little abashed.

"A coconut went through the wing a couple of days ago. I've not had time to repair it because of that problem with the fishtraps. Anyway, it's not equipped for night flying."

The mayor gave him a long, hard look.

"I hope my car's working," she said sarcastically.

"Of course," Brant answered, in a hurt voice. "All fueled up, and ready to go."

It was quite unusual for the mayor's car to go anywhere; one could walk the length of Tarna in twenty minutes, and all local transportation of food and equipment was handled by small sandrollers. In seventy years of official service the car had clocked up less than a hundred thousand kilometers and, barring accidents, should still be going strong for at least a century to come.

The Lassans had experimented cheerfully with most vices; but planned obsolescence and conspicuous consumption were not among them. No one could have guessed that the vehicle was older than any of its passengers as it started on the most historic journey it would ever make.

4. TOCSIN

No one heard the first tolling of Earth's funeral bell—not even the scientists who made the fatal discovery, far underground, in an abandoned Colorado gold mine.

It was a daring experiment, quite inconceivable before the mid-twentieth century. Once the neutrino had been detected, it was quickly realized that mankind had a new window on the universe. Something so penetrating that it passed through a planet as easily as light through a sheet of glass could be used to look into the hearts of suns.

Especially *the* Sun. Astronomers were confident that they understood the reactions powering the solar furnace, upon which all life on Earth ultimately depended. At the enormous pressures and temperatures at the Sun's core, hydrogen was fused to helium in a series of reactions that liberated vast amounts of energy. And, as an incidental by-product, neutrinos.

Finding the trillions of tons of matter in their way no more obstacle than a wisp of smoke, those solar neutrinos raced up from their birthplace at the velocity of light. Just two seconds later they emerged into space and spread outward across the universe. However many stars and planets they encountered, most of them would still have evaded capture by the insubstantial ghost of "solid" matter when Time itself came to an end.

Eight minutes after they had left the Sun, a tiny fraction of the solar torrent swept through the Earth—and an even smaller fraction was intercepted by the scientists in Colorado. They had buried their equipment more than a kilometer underground so that all the less penetrating radiations would be filtered out and they could trap the rare, genuine messengers from the heart of the Sun. By counting the captured neutrinos, they hoped to study in detail conditions at a spot that, as any philosopher could easily prove, was forever barred from human knowledge or observation.

The experiment worked; solar neutrinos were detected. But—*there were far too few of them*. There should have been three or four times as many as the massive instrumentation had succeeded in capturing.

Clearly, something was wrong, and during the 1970s the Case of the Missing Neutrinos escalated to a major scientific scandal. Equipment was checked and rechecked, theories were overhauled, and the experiment rerun scores of times—always with the same baffling result.

By the end of the twentieth century, the astrophysicists had been forced to accept a disturbing conclusion—though as yet no one realized its full implications.

There was nothing wrong with the theory, or with the equipment. The trouble lay inside the Sun.

The first secret meeting in the history of the International Astronomical Union took place in 2008 at Aspen, Colorado—not far from the scene of the original experiment, which had now been repeated in a dozen countries. A week later IAU Special Bulletin #55/08, bearing the deliberately low-key title "Some Notes on Solar Reactions," was in the hands of every government on Earth.

One might have thought that as the news slowly leaked out, the announcement of the End of the World would have produced a certain amount of panic. In fact, the general reaction was a stunned silence—then a shrug of the shoulders and the resumption of normal, everyday business.

Few governments had ever looked more than an election

14

ahead, few individuals beyond the lifetimes of their grand-children. And anyway, the astronomers might be wrong . . .

Even if humanity was under sentence of death, the date of execution was still indefinite. The Sun would not blow up for at least a thousand years; and who could weep for the fortieth generation?

5. NIGHT RIDE

Neither of the two moons had risen when the car set off along Tarna's most famous road, carrying Brant, Mayor Waldron, Councillor Simmons, and two senior villagers. Though he was driving with his usual effortless skill, Brant was still smouldering slightly from the mayor's reprimand. The fact that her plump arm was accidentally draped over his bare shoulders did little to improve matters.

But the peaceful beauty of the night and the hypnotic rhythm of the palm trees as they swept steadily through the car's moving fan of light quickly restored his normal good humor. And how could such petty personal feelings be allowed to intrude at such an historic moment as this?

In ten minutes, they would be at First Landing—and the beginning of their history. What was waiting for them there? Only one thing was certain; the visitor had homed on the still-operating beacon of the ancient seedship. It knew where to look, so it must be from some other human colony in this sector of space.

On the other hand—Brant was suddenly struck by a disturbing thought. Anyone—anything—could have detected that beacon, signaling to all the universe that Intelligence had once passed this way. He recalled that a few years ago there had been a move to switch off the transmission on the grounds that it served no useful purpose and might conceivably do harm. The motion had been rejected by a narrow margin for reasons that were sentimental and emotional rather than logical. Thalassa might soon regret that decision, but it was certainly much too late to do anything about it.

16

Councillor Simmons, leaning across from the backseat, was talking quietly to the mayor.

"Helga," he said—and it was the first time Brant had ever heard him use the mayor's first name—"do you think we'll still be able to communicate? Robot languages evolve very rapidly, you know."

Mayor Waldron didn't know, but she was very good at concealing ignorance.

"That's the least of our problems; let's wait until it arises. Brant—could you drive a little more slowly? I'd like to get there alive."

Their present speed was perfectly safe on this familiar road, but Brant dutifully slowed to forty klicks. He wondered if the mayor was trying to postpone the confrontation; it was an awesome responsibility, facing only the second outworld spacecraft in the history of the planet. The whole of Thalassa would be watching.

"Krakan!" one of the passengers swore in the backseat. "Did anybody bring a camera?"

"Too late to go back," Councillor Simmons answered. "Anyway, there will be plenty of time for photographs. I don't suppose they'll take off again right after saying hello!"

There was a certain mild hysteria in his voice, and Brant could hardly blame him. Who could tell *what* was waiting for them just over the brow of the next hill?

"I'll report just as soon as there's anything to tell you, Mr. President." Mayor Waldron was using the car radio. Brant had never even noticed the call; he had been too lost in a reverie of his own. For the first time in his life, he wished he had learned a little more history.

Of course, he was familiar enough with the basic facts; every child on Thalassa grew up with them. He knew how, as the centuries ticked remorsely by, the astronomers' diagnosis became ever more confident, the date of their prediction steadily more precise. In the year 3600, plus or minus seventy-five years, the Sun would become a nova. Not a very spectacular one—but big enough . . .

An old philosopher had once remarked that it settles a man's mind wonderfully to know that he will be hanged in the morning. Something of the same kind occurred with the entire human race during the closing years of the Fourth Millennium. If there was a single moment when humanity at last faced the truth with both resignation and determination, it was at the December midnight when the year 2999 changed to 3000. No one who saw that first 3 appear could forget that there would never be a 4.

Yet more than half a millennium remained; much could be done by the thirty generations that would still live and die on Earth as had their ancestors before them. At the very least, they could preserve the knowledge of the race and the greatest creations of human art.

Even at the dawn of the space age, the first robot probes to leave the Solar System had carried recordings of music, messages, and pictures in case they were ever encountered by other explorers of the cosmos. And though no sign of alien civilizations had ever been detected in the home galaxy, even the most pessimistic believed that intelligence must occur *somewhere* in the billions of other island universes that stretched as far as the most powerful telescope could see.

For centuries, terabyte upon terabyte of human knowledge and culture were beamed toward the Andromeda Nebula and its more distant neighbors. No one, of course, would ever know if the signals were received—or, if received, could be interpreted. But the motivation was one that most men could share; it was the impulse to leave some last message—some signal saying, "Look—I, too, was once alive!"

By the year 3000, astronomers believed that their giant orbiting telescopes had detected all planetary systems within five hundred light-years of the Sun. Dozens of approximately Earth-size worlds had been discovered, and some of the closer ones had been crudely mapped. Several had atmospheres bearing that unmistakable signature of life, an abnormally high percentage of oxygen. There was a reasonable chance that men could survive there—if they could reach them.

Men could not, but Man could.

The first seedships were primitive, yet even so they stretched technology to the limit. With the propulsion systems available by 2500, they could reach the nearest planetary system in two hundred years, carrying their precious burden of frozen embryos.

But that was the least of their tasks. They also had to carry the automatic equipment that would revive and rear these potential humans and teach them how to survive in an unknown but probably hostile environment. It would be useless—indeed, cruel—to decant naked, ignorant children on to worlds as unfriendly as the Sahara or the Antarctic. They had to be educated, given tools, shown how to locate and use local resources. After it had landed and the seedship became a Mother Ship, it might have to cherish its brood for generations.

Not only humans had to be carried but a complete *biota*. Plants (even though no one knew if there would be soil for them), farm animals, and a surprising variety of essential insects and microorganisms also had to be included in case normal food-production systems broke down and it was necessary to revert to basic agricultural techniques.

There was one advantage in such a new beginning. All the diseases and parasites that had plagued humanity since the beginning of time would be left behind, to perish in the sterilizing fire of Nova Solis.

Data banks, "expert systems" able to handle any conceivable situation, robots, repair and backup mechanisms—all these had to be designed and built. And they had to function over a time-span at least as long as that between the Declaration of Independence and the first landing on the Moon.

Though the task seemed barely possible, it was so inspiring that almost the whole of mankind united to achieve it. Here was a long-term goal—the *last* long-term goal—that could now give some meaning to life, even after Earth had been destroyed.

The first seedship left the Solar System in 2553, heading toward the Sun's near twin, Alpha Centauri A. Although the climate of the Earth-sized planet Pasadena was subject to violent extremes, owing to nearby Centauri B, the next likely target was more than twice as far away. The voyage time to Sirius X would be over four hundred years; when the seeder arrived, Earth might no longer exist.

But if Pasadena could be successfully colonized, there would be ample time to send back the good news. Two hundred years for the voyage, fifty years to secure a foothold and build a small transmitter, and a mere four years for the signal to get back to Earth—why, with luck, there would be shouting in the streets around the year 2800 . . .

In fact, it was 2786; Pasadena had done better than predicted. The news was electrifying and gave renewed encouragement to the seeding program. By this time, a score of ships had been launched, each with more advanced technology than its precursor. The latest models could reach a twentieth of the velocity of light, and more than fifty targets lay within their range.

Even when the Pasadena beacon became silent after beaming no more than the news of the initial landing, discouragement was only momentary. What had been done once could be done again—and yet again—with greater certainty of success.

By 2700 the crude technique of frozen embryos was abandoned. The genetic message that Nature encoded in the spiral structure of the DNA molecule could now be stored more easily, more safely, and even more compactly in the memories of the ultimate computers, so that a million genotypes could be carried in a seedship no larger than an ordinary thousand-passenger aircraft. An entire unborn nation, with all the replicating equipment needed to set up a new civilization, could be contained in a few hundred cubic meters and carried to the stars.

This, Brant knew, was what had happened on Thalassa seven hundred years ago. Already, as the road climbed up into the hills, they had passed some of the scars left by the first robot excavators as they sought the raw materials from which his own ancestors had been created. In a moment, they would see the long-abandoned processing plants and—

"What's *that*?" Councillor Simmons whispered urgently.

"Stop!" the mayor ordered. "Cut the engine, Brant." She reached for the car microphone.

"Mayor Waldron. We're at the seven-kilometer mark. There's a light ahead of us—we can see it through the trees— as far as I can tell, it's exactly at First Landing. We can't hear anything. Now we're starting up again."

Brant did not wait for the order but eased the speed control gently forward. This was the second most exciting thing that had happened to him in his entire life, next to being caught in the hurricane of '09.

That had been more than exciting; he had been lucky to escape alive. Perhaps there was also danger here, but he did not really believe so. Could robots be hostile? Surely there was nothing that any outworlders could possibly want from Thalassa except knowledge and friendship . . .

"You know," Councillor Simmons said, "I had a good view of the thing before it went over the trees, and I'm certain it was some kind of aircraft. Seedships never had wings and streamlining, of course. And it was very small."

"Whatever it is," Brant said, "we'll know in five minutes. Look at that light—it's come down in Earth Park—the obvious place. Should we stop the car and walk the rest of the way?"

Earth Park was the carefully tended oval of grass on the eastern side of First Landing, and it was now hidden from their direct view by the black, looming column of the Mother Ship, the oldest and most revered monument on the planet.

21

Spilling around the edges of the still-untarnished cylinder was a flood of light, apparently from a single brilliant source.

"Stop the car just before we reach the ship," the mayor ordered. "Then we'll get out and peek around it. Switch off your lights so they won't see us until we want them to."

"Them—or It?" asked one of the passengers, just a little hysterically. Everyone ignored him.

The car came to a halt in the ship's immense shadow, and Brant swung it around through a hundred and eighty degrees.

"Just so we can make a quick getaway," he explained, half seriously, half out of mischief; he still could not believe that they were in any real danger. Indeed, there were moments when he wondered if this was really happening. Perhaps he was still asleep and this was merely a vivid dream.

They got quietly out of the car and walked up to the ship, then circled it until they came to the sharply defined wall of light. Brant shielded his eyes and peered around the edge, squinting against the glare.

Councillor Simmons had been perfectly correct. It *was* some kind of aircraft—or aerospacecraft—and a very small one at that. Could the Northers?— No, that was absurd. There was no conceivable use for such a vehicle in the limited area of the Three Islands, and its development could not possibly have been concealed.

It was shaped like a blunt arrowhead and must have landed vertically, for there were no marks on the surrounding grass. The light came from a single source in a streamlined dorsal housing, and a small red beacon was flashing on and off just above that. Altogether, it was a reassuringly—indeed, disappointingly—ordinary machine. One that could not conceivably have traveled the dozen light-years to the nearest known colony.

Suddenly, the main light went out, leaving the little group of observers momentarily blind. When he recovered his night vision, Brant could see that there were windows in the forepart of the machine, glowing faintly with internal illumination. Why—it looked almost like a *manned* vehicle, not the robot craft they had taken for granted!

Mayor Waldron had come to exactly the same astonishing conclusion.

"It's not a robot—there are people in it! Let's not waste any more time. Shine your flashlight on me, Brant, so they can see us."

"Helga!" Councillor Simmons protested.

"Don't be an ass, Charlie. Let's go, Brant."

What was it that the first man on the Moon had said almost two millennia ago? "One small step . . ." They had taken about twenty when a door opened in the side of the vehicle, a double-jointed ramp flipped rapidly downward, and two humanoids walked out to meet them.

That was Brant's first reaction. Then he realized that he had been misled by the color of their skin—or what he could see of it through the flexible, transparent film that covered them from head to foot.

They were not humanoids—they were *human*. If he never went out into the sun again, he might become almost as bleached as they were.

The mayor was holding out her hands in the traditional "See—no weapons!" gesture as old as history.

"I don't suppose you'll understand me," she said, "but welcome to Thalassa."

The visitors smiled, and the older of the two—a handsome gray-haired man in his late sixties—held up his hands in response.

"On the contrary," he answered in one of the deepest and most beautifully modulated voices that Brant had ever heard, "we understand you perfectly. We're delighted to meet you."

For a moment, the welcoming party stood in stunned silence. But it was silly, thought Brant, to have been surprised. After all, they did not have the slightest difficulty understanding the speech of men who had lived two thousand years ago. When sound recording was invented, it froze the basic pho-

23

neme patterns of all languages. Vocabularies would expand, syntax and grammar might be modified—but pronunciation would remain stable for millennia.

Mayor Waldron was the first to recover.

"Well, that certainly saves a lot of trouble," she said rather lamely. "But where have you come from? I'm afraid we've lost touch with—our neighbors—since our deep-space antenna was destroyed."

The older man glanced at his much taller companion, and some silent message flashed between them. Then he again turned toward the waiting mayor.

There was no mistaking the sadness in that beautiful voice as he made his preposterous claim.

"It may be difficult for you to believe this," he said. "But we're not from any of the colonies. We've come straight from Earth."

II. MAGELLAN

6. PLANETFALL

Even before he opened his eyes, Loren knew exactly where he was, and he found this quite surprising. After sleeping for two hundred years, some confusion would have been understandable, but it seemed only yesterday that he had made his last entry in the ship's log. And as far as he could remember, he had not had a single dream. He was thankful for that.

Still keeping his eyes closed, he concentrated one at a time on all his other sense channels. He could hear a soft murmur of voices, quietly reassuring. There was the familiar sighing of the air exchangers, and he could feel a barely perceptible current wafting pleasant antiseptic smells across his face.

The one sensation he did not feel was that of weight. He lifted his right arm effortlessly: it remained floating in midair, awaiting his next order.

"Hello, Mister Lorenson," a cheerfully bullying voice said. "So you've condescended to join us again. How do you feel?"

Loren finally opened his eyes and tried to focus them on the blurred figure floating beside his bed.

"Hello . . . doctor. I'm fine. And hungry."

"That's always a good sign. You can get dressed—don't move too quickly for a while. And you can decide later if you want to keep that beard."

Loren directed his still-floating hand toward his chin; he was surprised at the amount of stubble he found there. Like the majority of men, he had never taken the option of permanent eradication—whole volumes of psychology had been written on *that* subject. Perhaps it was time to think about

27

doing so; amusing how such trivia cluttered up the mind, even at a moment like this.

"We've arrived safely?"

"Of course—otherwise you'd still be asleep. Everything's gone according to plan. The ship started to wake us a month ago—now we're in orbit above Thalassa. The maintenance crews have checked all the systems; now it's your turn to do some work. And we have a little surprise for you."

"A pleasant one, I hope."

"So do we. Captain Bey has a briefing two hours from now in Main Assembly. If you don't want to move yet, you can watch from here."

"I'll come to Assembly—I'd like to meet everyone. But can I have breakfast first? It's been a long time . . ."

Capt. Sirdar Bey looked tired but happy as he welcomed the fifteen men and women who had just been revived and introduced them to the thirty who formed the current A and B crews. According to ship's regulations, C crew was supposed to be sleeping—but several figures were lurking at the back of the Assembly room, pretending not to be there.

"I'm happy you've joined us," he told the newcomers. "It's good to see some fresh faces around here. And it's better still to see a planet and to know that our ship's carried out the first two hundred years of the mission plan without any serious anomalies. Here's Thalassa, right on schedule."

Everyone turned toward the visual display covering most of one wall. Much of it was devoted to data and state-of-ship information, but the largest section might have been a window looking out into space. It was completely filled by a stunningly beautiful image of a blue-white globe, almost fully illuminated. Probably everyone in the room had noticed the heartbreaking similarity to the Earth as seen from high above the Pacific—almost all water, with only a few isolated landmasses.

And there was land here—a compact grouping of three islands, partly hidden by a veil of cloud. Loren thought of Hawaii, which he had never seen and which no longer existed. But there was one fundamental difference between the two planets. The other hemisphere of Earth was mostly land; the other hemisphere of Thalassa was *entirely* ocean.

"There it is," the captain said proudly. "Just as the mission planners predicted. But there's one detail they didn't expect, which will certainly affect our operations.

"You'll recall that Thalassa was seeded by a Mark 3A fifty-thousand-unit module which left Earth in 2751 and arrived in 3109. Everything went well, and the first transmissions were received a hundred and sixty years later. They continued intermittently for almost two centuries, then suddenly stopped after a brief message reporting a major volcanic eruption. Nothing more was ever heard, and it was assumed that our colony on Thalassa had been destroyed—or at any rate reduced to barbarism as seems to have happened in several other cases.

"For the benefit of the newcomers, let me repeat what we've found. Naturally, we listened out on all frequencies when we entered the system. Nothing—not even power-system leakage radiation.

"When we got closer, we realized this didn't prove a thing. Thalassa has a very dense ionosphere. There might be a lot of medium- and short-wave chatter going on beneath it, and nobody outside would ever know. Microwaves would go through, of course, but maybe they don't need them, or we haven't been lucky enough to intercept a beam.

"Anyway, there's a well-developed civilization down there. We saw the lights of their cities—towns, at least—as soon as we had a good view of the nightside. There are plenty of small industries, a little coastal traffic—no large ships—and we've even spotted a couple of aircraft moving at all of five hundred klicks, which will get them anywhere in fifteen minutes.

"Obviously, they don't need much air transport in such a compact community, and they have a good system of roads. But we've still not been able to detect any communications.

And no satellites, either—not even meteorological ones, which you'd think they'd need . . . though perhaps not, as their ships probably never get out of sight of land. There's simply no other land to go to, of course.

"So there we are. It's an interesting situation—and a very pleasant surprise. At least I *hope* it will be. Now, any questions? Yes, Mister Lorenson?"

"Have we tried to contact them, sir?"

"Not yet; we thought it inadvisable until we know the exact level of their culture. Whatever we do, it may be a considerable shock."

"Do they know we're here?"

"Probably not."

"But surely—our drive—they must have seen *that!*"

It was a reasonable question, since a quantum ramjet at full power was one of the most dramatic spectacles ever contrived by man. It was as brilliant as an atomic bomb, and it lasted much longer—months instead of milliseconds.

"Possibly, but I doubt it. We were on the other side of the sun when we did most of our braking. They wouldn't have seen us in its glare."

Then someone asked the question that everybody had been thinking.

"Captain, how will this affect our mission?"

Sirdar Bey looked thoughtfully at the speaker.

"At this stage, it's still quite impossible to say. A few hundred thousand other humans—or whatever the population is—could make things a lot easier for us. Or at least much more pleasant. On the other hand, if they don't like us—"

He gave an expressive shrug.

"I've just remembered a piece of advice that an old explorer gave to one of his colleagues. If you assume that the natives are friendly, they usually are. And vice versa.

"So until they prove otherwise, we'll assume that they're friendly. And if they're not . . ."

The captain's expression hardened, and his voice became that of a commander who had just brought a great ship across fifty light-years of space.

"I've never claimed that might is right, but it's always very comforting to have it."

7. LORDS OF THE LAST DAYS

It was hard to believe that he was really and truly awake, and that life could begin again.

Lt. Comdr. Loren Lorenson knew that he could never wholly escape from the tragedy that had shadowed more than forty generations and had reached its climax in his own lifetime. During the course of his first new day, he had one continuing fear. Not even the promise, and mystery, of the beautiful ocean-world hanging there below *Magellan* could keep at bay the thought: what dreams will come when I close my eyes tonight in *natural* sleep for the first time in two hundred years?

He had witnessed scenes that no one could ever forget and which would haunt Mankind until the end of time. Through the ship's telescopes, he had watched the death of the Solar System. With his own eyes, he had seen the volcanoes of Mars erupt for the first time in a billion years; Venus briefly naked as her atmosphere was blasted into space before she herself was consumed; the gas giants exploding into incandescent fireballs. But these were empty, meaningless spectacles compared with the tragedy of Earth.

That, too, he had watched through the lenses of cameras that had survived a few minutes longer than the devoted men who had sacrificed the last moments of their lives to set them up. He had seen . . .

. . . the Great Pyramid glowing dully red before it slumped into a puddle of molten stone . . .

. . . the floor of the Atlantic, baked rock hard in seconds

before it was submerged again by the lava gushing from the volcanoes of the Mid-ocean Rift . . .

. . . the Moon rising above the flaming forests of Brazil and now itself shining almost as brilliantly as had the Sun, on its last setting, only minutes before . . .

. . . the continent of Antarctica emerging briefly after its long burial as the kilometers of ancient ice were burned away . . .

. . . the mighty central span of the Gibraltar Bridge melting even as it slumped downward through the burning air . . .

In that last century the Earth was haunted with ghosts— not of the dead but of those who now could never be born. For five hundred years the birthrate had been held at a level that would reduce the human population to a few million when the end finally came. Whole cities—even countries— had been deserted as mankind huddled together for History's closing act.

It was a time of strange paradoxes, of wild oscillations between despair and feverish exhilaration. Many, of course, sought oblivion through the traditional routes of drugs, sex, and dangerous sports—including what were virtually miniature wars, carefully monitored and fought with agreed weapons. Equally popular was the whole spectrum of electronic catharsis, from endless video games, interactive dramas, and direct stimulation of the brain's pleasure centers.

Because there was no longer any reason to take heed for the future on *this* planet, Earth's resources and the accumulated wealth of all the ages could be squandered with a clear conscience. In terms of material goods, all men were millionaires, rich beyond the wildest dreams of their ancestors, the fruits of whose toil they had inherited. They called themselves wryly, yet not without a certain pride, the Lords of the Last Days.

Yet though myriads sought forgetfulness, even more found satisfaction, as some men had always done, in working for goals beyond their own lifetimes. Much scientific research continued, using the immense resources that had now been freed. If a physicist needed a hundred tons of gold for an experiment, that was merely a minor problem in logistics, not budgeting.

Three themes dominated. First was the continual monitoring of the Sun—not because there was any remaining doubt but to predict the moment of detonation to the year, the day, the hour . . .

Second was the search for extraterrestrial intelligence, neglected after centuries of failure, now resumed with desperate urgency—and, even to the end, yielding no greater success than before. To all Man's questioning, the Universe still gave a dusty answer.

And the third, of course, was the seeding of the nearby stars in the hope that the human race would not perish with the dying of its Sun.

By the dawn of the final century, seedships of ever-increasing speed and sophistication had been sent to more than fifty targets. Most, as expected, had been failures, but ten had radioed back news of at least partial success. Even greater hopes were placed on the later and more advanced models, though they would not reach their distant goals until long after Earth had ceased to exist. The very last to be launched could cruise at a twentieth of the speed of light and would make planetfall in nine hundred and fifty years—if all went well.

Loren could still remember the launching of *Excalibur* from its construction cradle at the Lagrangian point between Earth and Moon. Though he was only five, even then he knew that this seedship would be the very last of its kind. But *why* the centuries-long program had been canceled just when it had reached technological maturity, he was still too young to understand. Nor could he have guessed how his own life would be changed by the stunning discovery that had transformed the entire situation and given mankind a new hope in the very last decades of terrestrial history.

Though countless theoretical studies had been made, no

one had ever been able to make a plausible case for *manned* spaceflight even to the nearest star. That such a journey might take a century was not the decisive factor; hibernation could solve that problem. A rhesus monkey had been sleeping in the Louis Pasteur satellite hospital for almost a thousand years and still showed perfectly normal brain activity. There was no reason to suppose that human beings could not do the same— though the record, held by a patient suffering from a peculiarly baffling form of cancer, was less than two centuries.

The biological problem had been solved; it was the engineering one that appeared insuperable. A vessel that could carry thousands of sleeping passengers, and all they needed for a new life on another world, would have to be as large as one of the great ocean liners that had once ruled the seas of Earth.

It would be easy enough to build such a ship beyond the orbit of Mars and using the abundant resources of the asteroid belt. However, it was impossible to devise engines that could get it to the stars in any reasonable length of time.

Even at a tenth of the speed of light, all the most promising targets were more than five hundred years away. Such a velocity had been attained by robot probes—flashing through nearby star systems and radioing back their observations during a few hectic hours of transit. But there was no way in which they could slow down for rendezvous or landing; barring accidents, they would continue speeding through the galaxy forever.

This was the fundamental problem with rockets—and no one had ever discovered any alternative for deep-space propulsion. It was just as difficult to lose speed as to acquire it, and carrying the necessary propellant for deceleration did not merely *double* the difficulty of a mission; it *squared* it.

A full-scale hibership could indeed be built to reach a tenth of the speed of light. It would require about a million tons of somewhat exotic elements as propellant; difficult but not impossible.

But in order to cancel that velocity at the end of the voyage, the ship must start not with a million—but a preposterous million, *million* tons of propellant. This, of course, was so completely out of the question that no one had given the matter any serious thought for centuries.

And then, by one of history's greatest ironies, Mankind was given the keys to the Universe—and barely a century in which to use them.

8. REMEMBRANCE OF LOVE LOST

How glad I am, thought Moses Kaldor, that I never succumbed to that temptation—the seductive lure that art and technology had first given to mankind more than a thousand years ago. Had I wished, I could have brought Evelyn's electronic ghost with me into exile, trapped in a few gigabytes of programming. She could have appeared before me, in any one of the backgrounds we both loved, and carried on a conversation so utterly convincing that a stranger could never have guessed that no one—*nothing*—was really there.

But I would have known after five or ten minutes unless I deluded myself by a deliberate act of will. And that I could never do. Though I am still not sure why my instincts revolt against it, I always refused to accept the false solace of a dialogue with the dead. I do not even possess, now, a simple recording of her voice.

It is far better this way, to watch her moving in silence in the little garden of our last home, knowing that this is no illusion of the image-makers but that it really *did* happen two hundred years ago on Earth.

And the only voice will be mine, here and now, speaking to the memory that still exists in my own human, living brain.

Private recording One. Alpha scrambler. Autoerase program.

You were right, Evelyn, and I was wrong. Even though I am the oldest man on the ship, it seems that I can still be useful.

37

When I awoke, Captain Bey was standing beside me. I felt flattered—as soon as I was able to feel anything.

"Well, Captain," I said, "this is quite a surprise. I half expected you to dump me in space as unnecessary mass."

He laughed and answered: "It could still happen, Moses; the voyage isn't over yet. But we certainly need you now. The Mission planners were wiser than you gave them credit."

"They listed me on the ship's manifest as quote Ambassador-Counsellor unquote. In which capacity am I required?"

"Probably both. And perhaps in your even better-known role as—"

"Don't hesitate if you wanted to say crusader, even though I never liked the word and never regarded myself as a leader of any movement. I only tried to make people think for themselves—I never wanted anyone to follow me blindly. History has seen too many leaders."

"Yes, but not all have been bad ones. Consider your namesake."

"Much overrated, though I can understand if you admire him. After all, you, too, have the task of leading homeless tribes into a promised land. I assume that some slight problem has arisen."

The captain smiled and answered: "I'm happy to see that you're fully alert. At this stage, there's not even a problem, and there's no reason why there should be. But a situation has arisen that no one expected, and you're our official diplomat. You have the one skill we never thought we'd need."

I can tell you, Evelyn, *that* gave me a shock. Captain Bey must have read my mind very accurately when he saw my jaw drop.

"Oh," he said quickly, "we haven't run into aliens! But it turns out that the human colony on Thalassa wasn't destroyed as we'd imagined. In fact, it's doing very well."

That, of course, was another surprise, though quite a pleasant one. Thalassa—the Sea, the Sea!—was a world I had never expected to set eyes upon. When *I* awoke, it should have been light-years behind and centuries ago.

"What are the people like? Have you made contact with them?"

"Not yet; that's your job. You know better than anyone else the mistakes that were made in the past. We don't want to repeat them here. Now, if you're ready to come up to the bridge, I'll give you a bird's-eye view of our long-lost cousins."

That was a week ago, Evelyn; how pleasant it is to have no time pressures after decades of unbreakable—and all too literal—deadlines! Now we know as much about the Thalassans as we can hope to do without actually meeting them face-to-face. And this we shall do tonight.

We have chosen common ground to show that we recognize our kinship. The site of the first landing is clearly visible and has been well kept, like a park—possibly a shrine. That's a very good sign: I only hope that *our* landing there won't be taken as sacrilege. Perhaps it will confirm that we are gods, which should make it easier for us. If the Thalassans have invented gods—that's one thing I want to find out.

I am beginning to live again, my darling. Yes, yes—you were wiser than I, the so-called philosopher! No man has a right to die while he can still help his fellows. It was selfish of me to have wished otherwise . . . to have hoped to lie forever beside you in the spot we had chosen so long ago, so far away . . . Now I can even accept the fact that you are scattered across the Solar System with all else that I ever loved on Earth.

But now there is work to be done; and while I talk to your memory, you are still alive.

9. THE QUEST FOR SUPERSPACE

Of all the psychological hammer blows that the scientists of the twentieth century had to endure, perhaps the most devastating—and unexpected—was the discovery that nothing was more crowded than "empty" space.

The old Aristotelian doctrine that Nature abhorred a vacuum was perfectly true. Even when every atom of seemingly solid matter was removed from a given volume, what remained was a seething inferno of energies of an intensity and scale unimaginable to the human mind. By comparison, even the most condensed form of matter—the hundred-million-tons-to-the-cubic-centimeter of a neutron star—was an impalpable ghost, a barely perceptible perturbation in the inconceivably dense, yet foamlike structure of "superspace."

That there was much more to space than naive intuition suggested was first revealed by the classic work of Lamb and Retherford in 1947. Studying the simplest of elements—the hydrogen atom—they discovered that something very odd happened when the solitary electron orbited the nucleus. Far from traveling in a smooth curve, it behaved as if being continually buffeted by incessant waves on a sub-submicroscopic scale. Hard though it was to grasp the concept, there were fluctuations *in the vacuum itself*.

Since the time of the Greeks, philosophers had been divided into two schools—those who believe that the operations of Nature flowed smoothly and those who argued that this was an illusion; everything really happened in discrete jumps or jerks too small to be perceptible in everyday life. The establishment of the atomic theory was a triumph for the second school of thought; and when Planck's Quantum Theory demonstrated that even light and energy came in little packets, not continuous streams, the argument finally ended.

In the ultimate analysis, the world of Nature was granular—discontinuous. Even if, to the naked human eye, a waterfall and a shower of bricks appeared very different, they were really much the same. The tiny "bricks" of H_2O were too small to be visible to the unaided senses, but they could be easily discerned by the instruments of the physicists.

And now the analysis was taken one step further. What made the granularity of space so hard to envisage was not only its sub-submicroscopic scale—but its sheer *violence*.

No one could really imagine a *million*th of a centimeter, but at least the number itself—a thousand thousands—was familiar in such human affairs as budgets and population statistics. To say that it would require a million viruses to span the distance of a centimeter did convey something to the mind.

But a million-*millionth* of a centimeter? That was comparable to the size of the electron, and already it was far beyond visualization. It could perhaps be grasped intellectually, but not emotionally.

And yet the scale of events in the structure of space was unbelievably smaller than this—so much so that, in comparison, an ant and an elephant were of virtually the same size. If one imagined it as a bubbling, foamlike mass (almost hopelessly misleading, yet a first approximation to the truth) then those bubbles were . . .

. . . a thousandth of a millionth of a millionth of a millionth of a millionth of a millionth . . .

. . . of a centimeter across.

And now imagine them continually exploding with energies comparable to those of nuclear bombs—and then reabsorbing that energy, and spitting it out again, and so on forever and forever.

This, in a grossly simplified form, was the picture that some late twentieth-century physicists had developed of the fundamental structure of space. That its intrinsic energies might ever be tapped must, at the time, have seemed completely ridiculous.

So, a lifetime earlier, had been the idea of releasing the newfound forces of the atomic nucleus; yet that had happened in less than half a century. To harness the "quantum fluctuations" that embodied the energies of space itself was a task orders of magnitude more difficult—and the prize correspondingly greater.

Among other things, it would give mankind the freedom of the universe. A spaceship could accelerate literally forever, since it would no longer need any fuel. The only practical limit to speed would, paradoxically, be that which the early aircraft had to contend with—the friction of the surrounding medium. The space between the stars contained appreciable quantities of hydrogen and other atoms, which could cause trouble long before one reached the ultimate limit set by the velocity of light.

The quantum drive might have been developed at any time after the year 2500, and the history of the human race would then have been very different. Unfortunately—as had happened many times before in the zigzag progress of science—faulty observations and erroneous theories delayed the final breakthrough for almost a thousand years.

The feverish centuries of the Last Days produced much brilliant—though often decadent—art but little new fundamental knowledge. Moreover, by that time the long record of failure had convinced almost everyone that tapping the energies of space was like perpetual motion, impossible even in theory, let alone in practice. However—unlike perpetual motion—it had not yet been *proved* to be impossible, and until this was demonstrated beyond all doubt, some hope still remained.

Only a hundred and fifty years before the end, a group of physicists in the Lagrange One zero-gravity research satellite announced that they had at last found such a proof; there were fundamental reasons why the immense energies of super-space, though they were real enough, could never be tapped. No one was in the least interested in this tidying up of an obscure corner of science.

A year later, there was an embarrassed cough from La-grange One. A slight mistake had been found in the proof. It was the sort of thing that had happened often enough in the past, though never with such momentous consequences.

A minus sign had been accidentally converted into a plus.

Instantly, the whole world was changed. The road to the stars had been opened up—five minutes before midnight.

III. SOUTH ISLAND

10. FIRST CONTACT

Perhaps I should have broken it more gently, Moses Kaldor told himself; they all seem in a state of shock. But that in itself is very instructive; even if these people are technologically backward (just look at that car!) they must realize that only a miracle of engineering could have brought us from Earth to Thalassa. First they will wonder how we did it, and then they will start to wonder *why*.

That, in fact, was the very first question that had occurred to Mayor Waldron. These two men in one small vehicle were obviously only the vanguard. Up there in orbit might be thousands—even millions. And the population of Thalassa, thanks to strict regulation, was already within ninety percent of ecological optimum . . .

"My name is Moses Kaldor," the older of the two visitors said. "And this is Lieutenant Commander Loren Lorenson, Assistant Chief Engineer, Starship *Magellan*. We apologize for these bubble suits—you'll realize that they are for our mutual protection. Though *we* come in friendship, our bacteria may have different ideas."

What a beautiful voice, Mayor Waldron told herself—as well she might. Once it had been the best known in the world, consoling—and sometimes provoking—millions in the decades before the End.

The mayor's notoriously roving eye did not, however, remain long on Moses Kaldor; he was obviously well into his sixties, and a little too old for her. The younger man was much more to her liking, though she wondered if she could ever really grow accustomed to that ugly white pallor. Loren Lor-

47

enson (what a charming name!) was nearly two meters in height, and his hair was so blond as to be almost silver. He was not as husky as—well, Brant—but he was certainly more handsome.

Mayor Waldron was a good judge both of men and of women, and she classified Lorenson very quickly. Here were intelligence, determination, perhaps even ruthlessness—she would not like to have him as an enemy, but she was certainly interested in having him as a friend. Or better . . .

At the same time, she did not doubt that Kaldor was a much *nicer* person. In his face and voice she could already discern wisdom, compassion, and also a profound sadness. Little wonder, considering the shadow under which he must have spent the whole of his life.

All the other members of the reception committee had now approached and were introduced one by one. Brant, after the briefest of courtesies, headed straight for the aircraft and began to examine it from end to end.

Loren followed him; he recognized a fellow engineer when he saw one and would be able to learn a good deal from the Thalassan's reactions. He guessed, correctly, what Brant's first question would be about. Even so, he was taken off balance.

"What's the propulsion system? Those jet orifices are ridiculously small—*if* that's what they are."

It was a very shrewd observation; these people were not the technological savages they had seemed at first sight. But it would never do to show that he was impressed. Better to counterattack and let him have it right between the eyes.

"It's a derated quantum ramjet, adapted for atmospheric flight by using air as a working fluid. Taps the Planck fluctuations—you know, ten to the minus thirty-three centimeters. So of course it has infinite range, in air or in space." Loren felt rather pleased with that "of course."

Once again he had to give Brant credit; the Lassan barely blinked and even managed to say, "Very interesting," as if he really meant it.

"Can I go inside?"

Loren hesitated. It might seem discourteous to refuse, and after all, they were anxious to make friends as quickly as possible. Perhaps more important, this would show who *really* had the mastery here.

"Of course," he answered. "But be careful not to touch anything." Brant was much too interested to notice the absence of "please."

Loren led the way into the spaceplane's tiny airlock. There was just enough room for the two of them, and it required complicated gymnastics to seal Brant into the spare bubble suit.

"I hope these won't be necessary for long," Loren explained, "but we have to wear them until the microbiology checks are complete. Close your eyes until we've been through the sterilization cycle."

Brant was aware of a faint violet glow, and there was a brief hissing of gas. Then the inner door opened, and they walked into the control cabin.

As they sat down side by side, the tough, yet scarcely visible films around them barely hindered their movements. Yet it separated them as effectively as if they were on different worlds—which, in many senses, they still were.

Brant was a quick learner, Loren had to admit. Give him a few hours and he could handle this machine—even though he would never be able to grasp the underlying theory. For that matter, legend had it that only a handful of men had ever *really* comprehended the geodynamics of superspace—and they were now centuries dead.

They quickly became so engrossed in technical discussions that they almost forgot the outside world. Suddenly, a slightly worried voice remarked from the general direction of the control panel, "Loren? Ship calling. What's happening? We've not heard from you for half an hour."

Loren reached lazily for a switch.

"Since you're monitoring us on six video and five audio

channels, that's a slight exaggeration." He hoped that Brant had got the message: We're in full charge of the situation, and we're not taking anything for granted. "Over to Moses—he's doing all the talking, as usual."

Through the curved windows, they could see that Kaldor and the mayor were still in earnest discussion, with Councillor Simmons joining in from time to time. Loren threw a switch, and their amplified voices suddenly filled the cabin, more loudly than if they had been standing beside them.

"—our hospitality. But you realize, of course, that this is an extraordinarily small world, as far as land surface is concerned. How many people did you say were aboard your ship?"

"I don't think I mentioned a figure, Madame Mayor. In any event, only a very few of us will ever come down to Thalassa, beautiful though it is. I fully understand your—ah—concern, but there's no need to feel the slightest apprehension. In a year or two, if all goes well, we'll be on our way again.

"At the same time, this isn't a social call—after all, we never expected to meet anyone here! But a starship doesn't delta-vee through half the velocity of light except for *very* good reasons. You have something that we need, and we have something to give you."

"What, may I ask?"

"From us, if you will accept it, the final centuries of human art and science. But I should warn you—consider what such a gift may do to your own culture. It might not be wise to accept everything we can offer."

"I appreciate your honesty—and your understanding. You must have treasures beyond price. What can we possibly offer in exchange?"

Kaldor gave his resonant laugh. "Luckily, *that's* no problem. You wouldn't even notice, if we took it without asking.

"All we want from Thalassa is a hundred thousand tons of water. Or, to be more specific, *ice*."

11. DELEGATION

The President of Thalassa had been in office for only two months and was still unreconciled to his misfortune. But there was nothing he could do about it except to make the best of a bad job for the three years it would last. Certainly it was no use demanding a recount; the selection program, which involved the generation and interleaving of thousand-digit random numbers, was the nearest thing to pure chance that human ingenuity could devise.

There were exactly five ways to avoid the danger of being dragged into the Presidential Palace (twenty rooms, one large enough to hold almost a hundred guests). You could be under thirty or over seventy; you could be incurably ill; you could be mentally defective; or you could have committed a grave crime. The only option really open to President Edgar Farradine was the last, and he had given it serious thought.

Yet he had to admit that despite the personal inconvenience it had caused him, this was probably the best form of government that mankind had ever devised. The mother planet had taken some ten thousand years to perfect it, by trial and often hideous error.

As soon as the entire adult population had been educated to the limits of its intellectual ability (and sometimes, alas, beyond), genuine democracy became possible. The final step required the development of instantaneous personal communications, linked with central computers. According to the historians, the first true democracy on Earth was established in the (Terran) year 2011, in a country called New Zealand.

Thereafter, selecting a head of state was relatively unimportant. Once it was universally accepted that anyone who *deliberately* aimed at the job should automatically be disqualified, almost any system would serve equally well, and a lottery was the simplest procedure.

"Mr. President," the Secretary to the Cabinet said, "the visitors are waiting in the library."

"Thank you, Lisa. And without their bubble suits?"

"Yes—all the medical people agree that it's perfectly safe. But I'd better warn you, sir. They—ah—*smell* a little odd."

"Krakan! In what way?"

The secretary smiled.

"Oh, it's not unpleasant—at least, *I* don't think so. It must be something to do with their food; after a thousand years, our biochemistries may have diverged. 'Aromatic' is probably the best word to describe it."

The president was not quite sure what that meant and was debating whether to ask when a disturbing thought occurred to him.

"And how," he said, "do you suppose we smell to *them*?"

To his relief, his five guests showed no obvious signs of olfactory distress when they were introduced, one at a time. But Secretary Elisabeth Ishihara was certainly wise to have warned him; now he knew exactly what the word "aromatic" implied. She was also correct in saying that it was not unpleasant; indeed, he was reminded of the spices his wife used when it was her turn to do the cooking in the palace.

As he sat down at the curve of the horseshoe-shaped conference table, the President of Thalassa found himself musing wryly about Chance and Fate—subjects that had never much concerned him in the past. But Chance, in its purest form, had put him in his present position. Now it—or its sibling, Fate—had struck again. How odd that *he*, an unambitious manufacturer of sporting equipment, had been chosen to preside at this historic meeting! Still, somebody had to do it; and he had to admit that he was beginning to enjoy himself. At the very least, no one could stop him from making his speech of welcome . . .

. . . It was, in fact, quite a good speech, though perhaps a little longer than necessary even for such an occasion as this. Toward the end he became aware that his listeners' politely attentive expressions were becoming a trifle glazed, so he cut out some of the productivity statistics and the whole section about the new power grid on South Island. When he sat down, he felt confident that he had painted a picture of a vigorous, progressive society with a high level of technical skills. Any superficial impressions to the contrary notwithstanding, Thalassa was neither backward nor decadent and still sustained the finest traditions of its great ancestors. Et cetera.

"Thank you very much, Mr. President," Captain Bey said in the appreciative pause that followed. "It was indeed a welcome surprise when we discovered that Thalassa was not only inhabited but flourishing. It will make our stay here all the more pleasant, and we hope to leave again with nothing but goodwill on both sides."

"Pardon me for being so blunt—it may even seem rude to raise the question just as soon as guests arrive—but how long *do* you expect to be here? We'd like to know as soon as possible so that we can make any necessary arrangements."

"I quite understand, Mr. President. We can't be specific at this stage, because it depends partly on the amount of assistance you can give us. My guess is at least one of your years—more probably two."

Edgar Farradine, like most Lassans, was not good at concealing his emotions, and Captain Bey was alarmed by the sudden gleeful—one might even say crafty—expression that spread across the chief executive's countenance.

"I hope, Your Excellency, that won't create any problems?" he asked anxiously.

"On the contrary," the president said, practically rubbing his hands. "You may not have heard, but our two hundredth Olympic Games are due in two years." He coughed modestly.

53

"I got a bronze in the thousand meters when I was a young man, so they've put me in charge of the arrangements. We could do with some competition from outside."

"Mr. President," the Secretary to the Cabinet said, "I'm not sure that the rules—"

"Which I make," the president continued firmly. "Captain, please consider this an invitation. Or a challenge, if you prefer."

The commander of the starship *Magellan* was a man accustomed to making swift decisions, but for once he was taken completely aback. Before he could think of a suitable reply, his chief medical officer stepped into the breach.

"That's extremely kind of you, Mr. President," Surgeon Commander Mary Newton said. "But as a medperson, may I point out that all of us are over thirty, we're completely out of training—and Thalassa's gravity is six percent stronger than Earth's, which would put us at a severe disadvantage. So unless your Olympics includes chess or card games . . ."

The president looked disappointed but quickly recovered.

"Oh, well—at least, Captain Bey, I'd like you to present some of the prizes."

"I'd be delighted," the slightly dazed commander said. He felt that the meeting was getting out of hand and determined to return to the agenda.

"May I explain what we hope to do here, Mr. President?"

"Of course" was the somewhat disinterested reply. His excellency's thoughts still seemed elsewhere. Perhaps he was still reliving the triumphs of his youth. Then, with an obvious effort, he focused his attention upon the present. "We were flattered, but rather puzzled, by your visit. There seems very little that our world can offer you. I'm told there was some talk of *ice*; surely that was a joke."

"No, Mr. President—we're absolutely serious. That's all we need of Thalassa, though now we've sampled some of your food products—I'm thinking especially of the cheese and wine

54

we had at lunch—we may increase our demands considerably. But *ice* is the essential; let me explain. First image, please."

The starship *Magellan*, two meters long, floated in front of the president. It looked so real that he wanted to reach out and touch it and would certainly have done so had there been no spectators to observe such naive behavior.

"You'll see that the ship is roughly cylindrical—length four kilometers, diameter one. Because our propulsion system taps the energies of space itself, there's no theoretical limit to speed, up to the velocity of light. But in practice, we run into trouble at about a fifth of that speed, owing to interstellar dust and gas. Tenuous though that is, an object moving through it at sixty thousand kilometers a second or more hits a surprising amount of material—and at that velocity even a single hydrogen atom can do appreciable damage.

"So *Magellan*, just like the first primitive spaceships, carries an ablation shield ahead of it. Almost any material would do as long as we use enough of it. And at the near-zero temperature between the stars, it's hard to find anything better than ice. Cheap, easily worked, and surprisingly strong! This blunt cone is what our little iceberg looked like when we left the Solar System two hundred years ago. And this is what it's like now."

The image flickered, then reappeared. The ship was unchanged, but the cone floating ahead of it had shrunk to a thin disc.

"That's the result of drilling a hole fifty light-years long through this rather dusty sector of the galaxy. I'm pleased to say the rate of ablation is within five percent of estimate, so we were never in any danger—though of course there was always the remote possibility that we might hit something *really* big. No shield could protect us against that—whether it was made of ice or the best armor-plate steel.

"We're still good for another ten light-years, but that's not enough. Our final destination is the planet Sagan Two— seventy-five lights to go.

55

"So now you understand, Mr. President, why we stopped at Thalassa. We would like to borrow—well, beg, since we can hardly promise to return it—a hundred or so thousand tons of water from you. We must build another iceberg, up there in orbit, to sweep the path ahead of us when we go on to the stars."

"How can we possibly help you to do that? Technically, you must be centuries ahead of us."

"I doubt it—except for the quantum drive. Perhaps Deputy Captain Malina can outline our plans—subject to your approval, of course."

"Please go ahead."

"First we have to locate a site for the freezing plant. There are many possibilities—it could be on any isolated stretch of coastline. It will cause absolutely no ecological disturbance, but if you wish, we'll put it on East Island—and hope that Krakan won't blow before we've finished!

"The plant design is virtually complete, needing only minor modifications to match whatever site we finally choose. Most of the main components can go into production right away. They're all very straightforward—pumps, refrigerating systems, heat exchangers, cranes—good old-fashioned Second Millennium Technology!

"If everything goes smoothly, we should have our first ice in ninety days. We plan to make standard-sized blocks, each weighing six hundred tons—flat, hexagonal plates—someone's christened them snowflakes, and the name seems to have stuck.

"When production's started, we'll lift one snowflake every day. They'll be assembled in orbit and keyed together to build up the shield. From first lift to final structural test should take two hundred fifty days. Then we'll be ready to leave."

When the deputy captain had finished, President Farradine sat in silence for a moment, a faraway look in his eye. Then he said, almost reverently. "Ice—I've never seen any, except at the bottom of a drink . . ."

As he shook hands with the departing visitors, President Farradine became aware of something strange. Their aromatic odor was now barely perceptible.

Had he grown accustomed to it already—or was he losing his sense of smell?

Although both answers were correct, around midnight he would have accepted only the second. He woke up with his eyes watering and his nose so clogged that it was difficult to breathe.

"What's the matter, dear?" Mrs. President asked anxiously.

"Call the—*atischoo!*—doctor," the chief executive answered. "Ours—*and* the one up in the ship. I don't believe there's a damn thing they can do, but I want to give them— *atischoo*—a piece of my mind. And I hope *you* haven't caught it, as well."

The president's lady started to reassure him but was interrupted by a sneeze.

They both sat up in bed and looked at each other unhappily.

"I believe it took seven days to get over it," sniffed the president. "But perhaps medical science has advanced in the last few centuries."

His hope was fulfilled, though barely. By heroic efforts, and with no loss of life, the epidemic was stamped out—in six miserable days.

It was not an auspicious beginning for the first contact between star-sundered cousins in almost a thousand years.

12. HERITAGE

We've been here two weeks, Evelyn—though it doesn't seem like it as that's only eleven of Thalassa's days. Sooner or later we'll have to abandon the old calendar, but my heart will always beat to the ancient rhythms of Earth.

It's been a busy time, and on the whole a pleasant one. The only real problem was medical; despite all precautions, we broke quarantine too soon, and about twenty percent of the Lassans caught some kind of virus. To make us feel even guiltier, none of *us* developed any symptoms whatsoever. Luckily, no one died, though I'm afraid we can't give the local doctors too much credit for that. Medical science is definitely backward here; they've grown to rely on automated systems so much that they can't handle anything out of the ordinary.

But we've been forgiven; the Lassans are very good-natured, easygoing people. They have been incredibly lucky—perhaps too lucky!—with their planet; it makes the contrast with Sagan Two even bleaker.

Their only real handicap is lack of land, and they've been wise enough to hold the population well below the sustainable maximum. If they're ever tempted to exceed it, they have the records of Earth's city-slums as a terrible warning.

Because they're such beautiful and charming people, it's a great temptation to help them instead of letting them develop their own culture in their own way. In a sense, they're our children—and all parents find it hard to accept that sooner or later they must cease to interfere.

To some extent, of course, we can't help interfering; our very presence does that. We're unexpected—though luckily not unwelcome—guests on their planet. And they can never forget that *Magellan* is orbiting just above the atmosphere, the last emissary from the world of their own ancestors.

I've revisited First Landing—*their* birthplace—and gone on the tour that every Lassan makes at least once in his life. It's a combination of museum and shrine, the only place on the whole planet to which the word "sacred" is remotely applicable. Nothing has changed in seven hundred years. The seed-ship, though it is now an empty husk, looks as if it has only just landed. All around it are the silent machines—the excavators and constructors and chemical processing plants with their robot attendants. And, of course, the nurseries and schools of Generation One.

There are almost no records of those first decades—perhaps deliberately. Despite all the skills and precautions of the planners, there must have been biological accidents, ruthlessly eliminated by the overriding program. And the time when those who had no organic parents gave way to those who did must have been full of psychological traumas.

But the tragedy and sadness of the Genesis Decades is now centuries in the past. Like the graves of all pioneers, it has been forgotten by the builders of the new society.

I would be happy to spend the rest of my life here; there's material on Thalassa for a whole army of anthropologists and psychologists and social scientists. Above all, how I wish I could meet some of my long-dead colleagues and let them know how many of our endless arguments have been finally resolved!

It *is* possible to build a rational and humane culture completely free from the threat of supernatural restraints. Though in principle I don't approve of censorship, it seems that those who prepared the archives for the Thalassan colony succeeded in an almost-impossible task. They purged the history and literature of ten thousand years, and the result has justified their efforts. We must be very cautious before replacing anything that was lost—however beautiful, however moving a work of art.

The Thalassans were never poisoned by the decay products of dead religions, and in seven hundred years no prophet has arisen here to preach a new faith. The very word "God" has almost vanished from their language, and they're quite surprised—or amused—when we happen to use it.

My scientist friends are fond of saying that one sample makes very poor statistics, so I wonder if the total lack of religion in this society really proves anything. We know that the Thalassans were also very carefully selected genetically to eliminate as many undesirable social traits as possible. Yes, yes—I know that only about fifteen percent of human behavior is determined by the genes—but that fraction is *very* important! The Lassans certainly seem remarkably free from such unpleasant traits as envy, intolerance, jealousy, anger. Is this entirely the result of cultural conditioning?

How I would love to know what happened to the seedships that were sent out by those religious groups in the twenty-sixth century! The Mormons' *Ark of the Covenant*, the *Sword of the Prophet*—there were half a dozen of them. I wonder if any of them succeeded, and if so, what part religion played in their success or their failure. Perhaps one day, when the local communications grid is established, we'll find what happened to those early pioneers.

One result of Thalassa's total atheism is a serious shortage of expletives. When a Lassan drops something on his toe, he's at a loss for words. Even the usual references to bodily functions aren't much help because they're all taken for granted. About the only general-purpose exclamation is "Krakan!" and that's badly overworked. But it does show what an impression Mount Krakan made when it erupted four hundred years ago; I hope I'll have a chance of visiting it before we leave.

That's still many months ahead, yet already I fear it. Not for the possible danger—if anything happens to the ship, I'll never know. But because it will mean that another link with Earth has been broken—and, my dearest, with you.

13. TASK FORCE

"The president's not going to like this," Mayor Waldron said with relish. "He's set his heart on getting you to North Island."

"I know," Deputy Captain Malina answered. "And we'll be sorry to disappoint him—he's been very helpful. But North Island's far too rocky; the only suitable coastal areas are already developed. Yet there's a completely deserted bay, with a gently sloping beach, only nine kilometers from Tarna—it will be perfect."

"Sounds too good to be true. *Why* is it deserted, Brant?"

"That was the Mangrove Project. All the trees died—we still don't know why—and no one's had the heart to tidy up the mess. It looks terrible, and smells worse."

"So it's already an ecological disaster area—you're welcome, Captain! You can only improve matters."

"I can assure you that our plant will be very handsome and won't damage the environment in the slightest. And of course it will all be dismantled when we leave. Unless you want to keep it."

"Thank you—but I doubt if we'd have much use for several hundred tons of ice a day. Meanwhile, what facilities can Tarna offer—accommodation, catering, transport?—we'll be happy to oblige. I assume that quite a number of you will be coming down to work here."

"Probably about a hundred, and we appreciate your offer of hospitality. But I'm afraid we'd be terrible guests: we'll be having conferences with the ship at all hours of the day and night. So we have to stick together—and as soon as we've

61

assembled our little prefabricated village, we'll move into it with all our equipment. I'm sorry if this seems ungracious—but any other arrangement simply wouldn't be practical."

"I suppose you're right." The mayor sighed. She had been wondering how she could bend protocol and offer what passed for the hospitality suite to the spectacular Lieutenant Commander Lorenson instead of to Deputy Captain Malina. The problem had appeared insoluble; now, alas, it would not even arise.

She felt so discouraged that she was almost tempted to call North Island and invite her last official consort back for a vacation. But the wretch would probably turn her down again, and she simply couldn't face that.

14. MIRISSA

Even when she was a very old woman, Mirissa Leonidas could still remember the exact moment when she first set eyes on Loren. There was no one else—not even Brant—of which this was true.

Novelty had nothing to do with it; she had already met several of the Earthmen before encountering Loren, and they had made no unusual impression on her. Most of them could have passed as Lassans if they had been left out in the sun for a few days.

But not Loren; his skin never tanned, and his startling hair became, if anything, even more silvery. That was certainly what had first drawn her notice as he was emerging from Mayor Waldron's office with two of his colleagues—all of them bearing that slightly frustrated look that was the usual outcome of a session with Tarna's lethargic and well-entrenched bureaucracy.

Their eyes had met, but for a moment only. Mirissa took a few more paces; then, without any conscious volition, she came to a dead halt and looked back over her shoulder—to see that the visitor was staring at her. Already, they both knew that their lives had been irrevocably changed.

Later that night, after they had made love, she asked Brant, "Have they said how long they're staying?"

"You do choose the worst times," he grumbled sleepily. "At least a year. Maybe two. Good night—*again*."

She knew better than to ask any more questions even though she still felt wide awake. For a long time she lay open-eyed, watching the swift shadows of the inner moon sweep across the floor while the cherished body beside her sank gently into sleep.

She had known not a few men before Brant, but since they had been together, she had been utterly indifferent to anyone else. Then why this sudden interest—she still pretended it was no stronger than that—in a man she had glimpsed only for a few seconds and whose very name she did not even know? (Though that would certainly be one of tomorrow's first priorities.)

Mirissa prided herself on being honest and clear-sighted; she looked down on women—or men—who let themselves be ruled by their emotions. Part of the attraction, she was quite sure, was the element of novelty, the glamour of vast new horizons. To be able to speak to someone who had actually walked through the cities of Earth—had witnessed the last hours of the Solar System—and was now on the way to new suns was a wonder beyond her wildest dreams. It made her once more aware of that underlying dissatisfaction with the placid tempo of Thalassan life despite her happiness with Brant.

Or was it merely contentment and not true happiness? What did she *really* want? Whether she could find it with these strangers from the stars, she did not know, but before they left Thalassa forever, she meant to try.

That same morning, Brant had also visited Mayor Waldron, who greeted him with slightly less than her usual warmth when he dumped the fragments of his fish-trap on her desk.

"I know you've been busy with more important matters," he said, "but what are we going to do about *this*?"

The mayor looked without enthusiasm at the tangled mess of cables. It was hard to focus on the day-to-day routine after the heady excitements of interstellar politics.

"What do *you* think happened?" she asked.

"It's obviously deliberate—see how this wire was twisted until it broke. Not only was the grid damaged, but sections have been taken away. I'm sure no one on South Island would do such a thing. What motive would they have? And I'd be bound to find out sooner or later . . ."

Brant's pregnant pause left no doubt as to what would happen then.

"Who do you suspect?"

"Ever since I started experimenting with electric trapping, I've been fighting not only the Conservers but those crazy people who believe that *all* food should be synthetic because it's wicked to eat living creatures, like animals—or even plants."

"The Conservers, at least, may have a point. If your trap is as efficient as you claim, it could upset the ecological balance they're always talking about."

"The regular reef census would tell us if *that* was happening, and we'd just switch off for a while. Anyway, it's the pelagics I'm really after; my field seems to attract them from up to three or four kilometers away. And even if everyone on the Three Islands ate nothing but fish, we couldn't make a dent in the oceanic population."

"I'm sure you're right—as far as the indigenous pseudofish are concerned. And much good that does, since most of them are too poisonous to be worth processing. Are you *sure* that the Terran stock has established itself securely? You might be the last straw, as the old saying goes."

Brant looked at the mayor with respect; she was continually surprising him with shrewd questions like this. It never occurred to him that she would not have held her position for so long if there was not a great deal more in her than met the eye.

"I'm afraid the tuna aren't going to survive; it will be a few billion years before the oceans are salty enough for them. But the trout and salmon are doing very well."

"And they're certainly delicious; they might even overcome the moral scruples of the Synthesists. Not that I really accept

65

your interesting theory. Those people may talk, but they don't *do* anything."

"They released a whole herd of cattle from that experimental farm a couple of years ago."

"You mean they *tried* to—the cows walked straight home again. Everyone laughed so much that they called off any further demonstrations. I simply can't imagine that they'd go to all this trouble." She gestured toward the broken grid.

"It wouldn't be difficult—a small boat at night, a couple of divers—the water's only twenty meters deep."

"Well, I'll make some inquiries. Meanwhile, I want you to do two things."

"What?" Brant said, trying not to sound suspicious and failing completely.

"Repair the grid—Tech Stores will give you anything you need. And stop making any more accusations until you're one hundred percent certain. If you're wrong, you'll look foolish and may have to apologize. If you're right, you may scare the perpetrators away before we can catch them. Understand?"

Brant's jaw dropped slightly: he had never seen the mayor in so incisive a mood. He gathered up Exhibit A and made a somewhat chastened departure.

He might have been even more chastened—or perhaps merely amused—to know that Mayor Waldron was no longer quite so enamored of him.

Assistant Chief Engineer Loren Lorenson had impressed more than one of Tarna's citizens that morning.

15. TERRA NOVA

Such a reminder of Earth was an unfortunate name for the settlement, and no one admitted responsibility. But it was slightly more glamorous than "base camp," and was quickly accepted.

The complex of prefabricated huts had shot up with astonishing speed—literally overnight. It was Tarna's first demonstration of Earthpersons—or rather Earth robots—in action, and the villagers were hugely impressed. Even Brant, who had always considered that robots were more trouble than they were worth, except for hazardous or monotonous work, began to have second thoughts. There was one elegant general-purpose mobile constructor that operated with such blinding speed that it was often impossible to follow its movements. Wherever it went, it was followed by an admiring crowd of small Lassans. When they got in its way, it politely stopped whatever it was doing until the coast was clear. Brant decided that this was exactly the kind of assistant he needed; perhaps there was some way he could persuade the visitors . . .

By the end of a week, Terra Nova was a fully functioning microcosm of the great ship orbiting beyond the atmosphere. There was plain but comfortable accommodation for a hundred crewmembers, with all the life-support systems they needed—as well as library, gymnasium, swimming pool, and theater. The Lassans approved of these facilities and hastened to make full use of them. As a result, the population of Terra Nova was usually at least double the nominal one hundred.

Most of the guests—whether invited or not—were anxious

67

to help and determined to make their visitors' stay as comfortable as possible. Such friendliness, though very welcome and much appreciated, was often embarrassing. The Lassans were insatiably inquisitive, and the concept of privacy was almost unknown to them. A Please Do Not Disturb sign was often regarded as a personal challenge, which led to interesting complications . . .

"You're all senior officers and highly intelligent adults," Captain Bey had said at the last staff conference aboard ship. "So it shouldn't be necessary to tell you this. Try not to get involved in any, ah, entanglements until we know *exactly* how the Lassans think about such matters. They appear very easygoing, but that could be deceptive. Don't you agree, Dr. Kaldor?"

"I can't pretend, Captain, to be an authority on Lassan *mores* after so short a period of study. But there are some interesting historical parallels, when the old sailing-ships on Earth put to port after long sea voyages—I expect many of you have seen that classic video antique, *Mutiny on the Bounty*."

"I trust, Dr. Kaldor, that you're not comparing me to Captain Cook—I mean Bligh."

"It wouldn't be an insult; the real Bligh was a brilliant seaman, and most unfairly maligned. At this stage, all we need are common sense, good manners—and, as you indicated, caution."

Had Kaldor looked in *his* direction, Loren wondered, when he made that remark? Surely it was not already so obvious . . .

After all, his official duties put him in contact with Brant Falconer a dozen times a day. There was no way he could avoid meeting Mirissa—even if he wished to.

They had never yet been alone together and had still exchanged no more than a few words of polite conversation. But already there was no need to say anything more.

16. PARTY GAMES

"It's called a baby," Mirissa said, "and despite appearances, one day it will grow up into a perfectly normal human being."

She was smiling, yet there was moisture in her eyes. It had never occurred to her until she noticed Loren's fascination that there were probably more children in the little village of Tarna than there had been on the entire planet Earth during the final decades of virtually zero birthrate.

"Is it . . . yours?" he asked quietly.

"Well, first of all it's not an *it*; it's a he. Brant's nephew, Lester—we're looking after him while his parents are on North Island."

"He's beautiful. Can I hold him?"

As if on cue, Lester started to wail.

"That wouldn't be a good idea." Mirissa laughed, scooping him up hastily and heading toward the nearest bathroom. "I recognize the signals. Let Brant or Kumar show you around while we're waiting for the other guests."

The Lassans loved parties and missed no opportunity for arranging them. The arrival of *Magellan* was, quite literally, the chance of a lifetime—indeed, of many lifetimes. If they had been rash enough to accept all the invitations they received, the visitors would have spent every waking moment staggering from one official or unofficial reception to another. None too soon, the captain had issued one of his infrequent but implacable directives—"Bey thunderbolts," or simply "Beybolts," as they were wryly called—rationing his officers to a maximum of one party per five days. There were some who considered that, in view of the time it often took to recover from Lassan hospitality, this was much too generous.

The Leonidas residence, currently occupied by Mirissa, Kumar, and Brant, was a large ring-shaped building that had been the family's home for six generations. One story high—there were few upper floors in Tarna—it enclosed a grass-covered patio about thirty meters across. At the very center was a small pond complete with a tiny island accessible by a picturesque wooden bridge. And on the island was a solitary palm-tree that did not seem to be in the best of health.

"They have to keep replacing it," Brant said apologetically. "Some Terran plants do very well here—others just fade away despite all the chemical boosters we give them. It's the same problem with the fish we've tried to introduce. Freshwater farms work fine, of course, but we don't have space for them. It's frustrating to think that there's a million times as much ocean, if only we could use it properly."

In Loren's private opinion, Brant Falconer was something of a bore when he started talking about the sea. He had to admit, however, that it was a safer subject of conversation than Mirissa, who had now managed to get rid of Lester and was greeting the new guests as they arrived.

Could he ever have dreamed, Loren asked himself, that he would find himself in a situation like this? He had been in love before, but the memories—even the names—were mercifully blurred by the erasing programs they had all undergone before leaving the Solar System. He would not even attempt to recapture them; why torment himself with images from a past that had been utterly destroyed?

Even Kitani's face was blurring, though he had seen her in the hibernaculum only a week ago. She was part of a future they had planned but might never share: Mirissa was here and now—full of life and laughter, not frozen in half a millennium of sleep. She had made him feel whole once more, joyful in the knowledge that the strain and exhaustion of the Last Days had not, after all, robbed him of his youth.

Every time they were together, he felt the pressure that told him he was a man again; until it had been relieved, he would know little peace and would not even be able to perform his work efficiently. There had been times when he had seen Mirissa's face superimposed on the Mangrove Bay plans and flow diagrams and had been forced to give the computer a PAUSE command before they could continue their joint mental conversation. It was a peculiarly exquisite torture to spend a couple of hours within meters of her, able to exchange no more than polite trivialities.

To Loren's relief, Brant suddenly excused himself and hurried away. Loren quickly discovered the reason.

"Commander Lorenson!" Mayor Waldron said. "I hope Tarna's been treating you well."

Loren groaned inwardly. He knew that he was supposed to be polite to the mayor, but the social graces had never been his strong point.

"Very well, thank you. I don't believe you've met these gentlemen—"

He called, much more loudly than was really necessary, across the patio to a group of colleagues who had just arrived. By good luck, they were all lieutenants; even off duty, rank had its privileges, and he never hesitated to use it.

"Mayor Waldron, this is Lieutenant Fletcher—your first time down, isn't it Owen? Lieutenant Werner Ng, Lieutenant Ranjit Winson, Lieutenant Karl Bosley . . ."

Just like the clannish Martians, he thought, always sticking together. Well, that made them a splendid target, and they were a personable group of young men. He did not believe that the mayor even noticed when he made his strategic withdrawal.

Doreen Chang would have much preferred to talk to the captain, but he had made a high-velocity, token appearance, downed one drink, apologized to his hosts, and departed.

"Why won't he let me interview him?" she asked Kaldor,

71

who had no such inhibitions and had already logged several days' worth of audio and video time.

"Captain Sirdar Bey," he answered, "is in a privileged position. Unlike the rest of us, he doesn't have to explain—or to apologize."

"I detect a note of mild sarcasm in your voice," the Thalassa Broadcasting Corporation's star newsperson said.

"It wasn't intended. I admire the captain enormously and even accept his opinion of me—with reservations, of course. Er—are you recording?"

"Not *now*. Too much background noise."

"Lucky for you I'm such a trusting person, since there's no way I could tell if you were."

"Definitely off the record, Moses. What *does* he think of you?"

"He's glad to have my views, and my experience, but he doesn't take me very seriously. I know exactly why. He once said, 'Moses—you like power but not responsibility. I enjoy both.' It was a very shrewd statement; it sums up the difference between us."

"How did you answer?"

"What could I say? It was perfectly true. The only time I got involved in practical politics was—well, not a disaster, but I never really enjoyed it."

"The Kaldor Crusade?"

"Oh—you know about that. Silly name—it annoyed me. And that was another point of disagreement between the captain and myself. He thought—still thinks, I'm sure—the Directive ordering us to avoid *all* planets with life-potential is a lot of sentimental nonsense. Another quote from the good captain: 'Law I understand. Metalaw is bal—'er, balderdash."

"This is fascinating—one day you must let me record it."

"Definitely not. What's happening over there?"

Doreen Chang was a persistent lady, but she knew when to give up.

"Oh, that's Mirissa's favorite gas-sculpture. Surely you had them on Earth."

"Of course. And since we're still off the record, I don't think it's art. But it's amusing."

The main lights had been switched off in one section of the patio, and about a dozen guests had gathered around what appeared to be a very large soap bubble, almost a meter in diameter. As Chang and Kaldor walked toward it, they could see the first swirls of color forming inside, like the birth of a spiral nebula.

"It's called 'Life,'" Doreen said, "and it's been in Mirissa's family for two hundred years. But the gas is beginning to leak; I can remember when it was much brighter."

Even so, it was impressive. The battery of electron guns and lasers in the base had been programmed by some patient, long-dead artist to generate a series of geometrical shapes that slowly evolved into organic structures. From the center of the sphere, ever more complex forms appeared, expanded out of sight, and were replaced by others. In one witty sequence, single-celled creatures were shown climbing a spiral staircase, recognizable at once as a representation of the DNA molecule. With each step, something new was added; within a few minutes, the display had encompassed the four-billion-year odyssey from amoeba to man.

Then the artist tried to go beyond, and Kaldor lost him. The contortions of the fluorescent gas became too complex and too abstract. Perhaps if one saw the display a few more times, a pattern would emerge—

"What happened to the sound?" Doreen asked when the bubble's maelstrom of seething colors abruptly winked out. "There used to be some very good music, especially at the end."

"I was afraid someone would ask that question," Mirissa said with an apologetic smile. "We're not certain whether the trouble is in the playback mechanism or the program itself."

"Surely you have a backup!"

73

"Oh, yes, of course. But the spare module is somewhere in Kumar's room, probably buried under bits of his canoe. Until you've seen his den, you won't understand what entropy really means."

"It's not a canoe—it's a kayak," protested Kumar, who had just arrived with a pretty local girl clinging to each arm. "And what's entropy?"

One of the young Martians was foolish enough to attempt an explanation by pouring two drinks of different colors into the same glass. Before he could get very far, his voice was drowned by a blast of music from the gas-sculpture.

"You see!" Kumar shouted above the din, with obvious pride. "Brant can fix *anything!*"

Anything? thought Loren. I wonder . . . I wonder . . .

17. CHAIN OF COMMAND

From: Captain
To: All Crew Members

CHRONOLOGY

As there has already been a great deal of unnecessary confusion in this matter, I wish to make the following points:

1. All Ship's records and schedules will remain on Earth Time—corrected for relativistic effects—until the end of the voyage. All clocks and timing systems aboard ship will continue to run on ET.

2. For convenience, ground crews will use Thalassan time (TT) when necessary, but will keep all records in ET with TT in parenthesis.

3. To remind you:

The duration of the Thalassan Mean Solar Day is 29.4325 hours ET.

There are 313.1561 Thalassan days in the Thalassan Sidereal Year, which is divided into 11 months of 28 days. January is omitted from the calendar, but the five extra days to make up the total of 313 follow immediately after the last day (28th) of December. Leap days are intercalated every six years, but there will be none during our stay.

4. Since the Thalassan day is 22% longer than Earth's, and the number of those days in its year is 14% shorter, the actual length of the Thalassan year is only about 5% longer than Earth's. As you are all

aware, this has one practical convenience, in the matter of birthdays. Chronological age means almost the same on Thalassa as on Earth. A 20-year-old Thalassan has lived as long as a 21-year-old Earthperson. The Lassan calendar starts at First Landing, which was 3109 ET. The current year is 718TT or 754 Earth years later.

5. Finally—and we can also be thankful for this— there is only one Time Zone to worry about on Thalassa.

Sirdar Bey (Capt.)
3863.02.27.21.30 ET
718.00.02.15.00 TT

"Who would have thought anything so simple could be so complicated!" Mirissa laughed when she had scanned the printout pinned up on the Terra Nova bulletin board. "I suppose this is one of the famous Beybolts. What sort of man is the captain? I've never had a real chance of talking to him."

"He's not an easy person to know," Moses Kaldor answered. "I don't think I've spoken to him in private more than a dozen times. And he's the only man on the ship who everyone calls 'Sir'—*always*. Except maybe Deputy Captain Malina, when they're alone together . . . Incidentally, that notice was certainly not a genuine Beybolt—it's too technical. Science Officer Varley and Secretary LeRoy must have drafted it. Captain Bey has a remarkable grasp of engineering principles—much better than I do—but he's primarily an administrator. And occasionally, when he has to be, commander-in-chief."

"I'd hate his responsibility."

"It's a job someone has to do. Routine problems can usually be solved by consulting the senior officers and the computer banks. But sometimes a decision has to be made by a single individual, who has the authority to enforce it. That's why you need a captain. You can't run a ship by a committee—at least not all the time."

"I think that's the way we run Thalassa. Can you imagine President Farradine as captain of *anything*?"

"These peaches are delicious," Kaldor said tactfully, helping himself to another, though he knew perfectly well that they had been intended for Loren. "But you've been lucky; you've had no real crises for seven hundred years! Didn't one of your own people once say: 'Thalassa has no history—only statistics?'"

"Oh, that's not true! What about Mount Krakan?"

"That was a natural disaster—and hardly a major one. I'm referring to, ah, political crises: civil unrest, *that* sort of thing."

"We can thank Earth for that. You gave us a Jefferson Mark Three Constitution—someone once called it utopia in two megabytes—and it's worked amazingly well. The program hasn't been modified for three hundred years. We're still only on the Sixth Amendment."

"And long may you stay there," Kaldor said fervently. "I should hate to think that we were responsible for a seventh."

"If that happens, it will be processed first in the Archives memory banks. When are you coming to visit us again? There are so many things I want to show you."

"Not as many as I want to see. You must have so much that will be useful for us on Sagan Two, even though it's a very different kind of world." And a far less attractive one, he added to himself.

While they were talking, Loren had come quietly into the reception area, obviously on his way from the games room to the showers. He was wearing the briefest of shorts and had a towel draped over his bare shoulders. The sight left Mirissa distinctly weak at the knees.

"I suppose you've beaten everyone, as usual," Kaldor said. "Doesn't it get boring?"

Loren gave a wry grin.

"Some of the young Lassans show promise. One's just taken three points off me. Of course, I was playing with my left hand."

"In the very unlikely event he hasn't already told you," Kaldor remarked to Mirissa, "Loren was once table-tennis champion of Earth."

"Don't exaggerate, Moses. I was only about number five—and standards were miserably low toward the end. Any Third Millennium Chinese player would have pulverized me."

"I don't suppose you've thought of teaching Brant," Kaldor said mischievously. "That should be interesting."

There was a brief silence. Then Loren answered, smugly but accurately, "It wouldn't be fair."

"As it happens," Mirissa said, "Brant would like to show *you* something."

"Oh?"

"You said you've never been on a boat."

"That's true."

"Then you have an invitation to join Brant and Kumar at Pier Three—eight-thirty tomorrow morning."

Loren turned to Kaldor.

"Do you think it's safe for me to go?" he asked in mock seriousness. "I don't know how to swim."

"I shouldn't worry," Kaldor answered helpfully. "If they're planning a one-way trip for you, that won't make the slightest difference."

18. KUMAR

Only one tragedy had darkened Kumar Leonidas's eighteen years of life; he would always be ten centimeters shorter than his heart's desire. It was not surprising that his nickname was "The Little Lion"—though very few dared use it to his face.

To compensate for his lack of height, he had worked assiduously on width and depth. Many times Mirissa had told him, in amused exasperation, "Kumar—if you spent as much time building your brain as your body, you'd be the greatest genius on Thalassa." What she had never told him—and scarcely admitted even to herself—was that the spectacle of his regular morning exercises often aroused most unsisterly feelings in her breast as well as a certain jealously of all the other admirers who had gathered to watch. At one time or other this had included most of Kumar's age group. Although the envious rumor that he had made love to all the girls and half the boys in Tarna was wild hyperbole, it did contain a considerable element of truth.

But Kumar, despite the intellectual gulf between him and his sister, was no muscle-bound moron. If anything really interested him, he would not be satisfied until he had mastered it, no matter how long that took. He was a superb seaman and for over two years, with occasional help from Brant, had been building an exquisite four-meter kayak. The hull was complete, but he had not yet started on the deck.

One day, he swore, he was going to launch it, and everyone would stop laughing. Meanwhile, the phrase "Kumar's kayak" had come to mean any unfinished job around Tarna—of which, indeed, there were a great many.

Apart from this common Lassan tendency to procrastinate, Kumar's chief defects were an adventurous nature and a fondness for sometimes risky practical jokes. This, it was widely believed, would someday get him into serious trouble.

But it was impossible to be angry with even his most outrageous pranks, for they lacked all malice. He was completely open, even transparent; no one could ever imagine his telling a lie. For this, he could be forgiven much, and frequently was.

The arrival of the visitors had, of course, been the most exciting event in his life. He was fascinated by their equipment, the sound, video, and sensory recordings they had brought, the stories they told—everything about them. And because he saw more of Loren than any of the others, it was not surprising that Kumar attached himself to him.

This was not a development that Loren altogether appreciated. If there was one thing even more unwelcome than an inconvenient mate, it was that traditional spoilsport, an adhesive kid brother.

19. PRETTY POLLY

"I still can't believe it, Loren," Brant Falconer said. "You've *never* been in a boat—or on a ship?"

"I seem to remember paddling a rubber dinghy across a small pond. That would have been when I was about five years old."

"Then you'll enjoy this. Not even a swell to upset your stomach. Perhaps we can persuade you to dive with us."

"No, thanks—I'll take one new experience at a time. And I've learned never to get in the way when other men have work to do."

Brant was right; he *was* beginning to enjoy himself as the hydrojets drove the little trimaran almost silently out toward the reef. Yet soon after he had climbed aboard and seen the firm safety of the shoreline rapidly receding, he had known a moment of near panic.

Only a sense of the ridiculous had saved him from making a spectacle of himself. He had traveled fifty light-years—the longest journey ever made by human beings—to reach this spot. And now he was worried about the few hundred meters to the nearest land.

Yet there was no way in which he could turn down the challenge. As he lay at ease in the stern, watching Falconer at the wheel (how had he acquired that white scar across his shoulders?—oh, yes, he had mentioned something about a crash in a microflyer, years ago . . .), he wondered just what was going through the Lassan's mind.

It was hard to believe that any human society, even the most enlightened and easygoing, could be totally free from jealousy or some form of sexual possessiveness. Not that there was—so far, alas!—much for Brant to be jealous about.

Loren doubted if he had spoken as many as a hundred words to Mirissa; most of them had been in the company of her husband. Correction: On Thalassa, the terms husband and wife were not used until the birth of the first child. When a son was chosen, the mother usually—but not invariably—assumed the name of the father. If the firstborn was a girl, both kept the mother's name—at least until the birth of the second, and final, child.

There were very few things indeed that shocked the Lassans. Cruelty—especially to children—was one of them. And having a third pregnancy, on this world with only twenty thousand square kilometers of land, was another.

Infant mortality was so low that multiple births were sufficient to maintain a steady population. There had been one famous case—the only one in the whole history of Thalassa—when a family had been blessed, or afflicted, with double quintuplets. Although the poor mother could hardly be blamed, her memory was now surrounded with that aura of delicious depravity that had once enveloped Lucrezia Borgia, Messalina, or Faustine.

I'll have to play my cards very, very carefully, Loren told himself. That Mirissa found him attractive, he already knew. He could read it in her expression and in the tone of her voice. And he had even stronger proof in accidental contacts of hand and soft collisions of body that had lasted longer than were strictly necessary.

They both knew that it was only a matter of time. And so, Loren was quite sure, did Brant. Yet despite the mutual tension between them, they were still friendly enough.

The pulsation of the jets died away, and the boat drifted to a halt, close to a large glass buoy that was gently bobbing up and down in the water.

"That's our power supply," Brant said. "We only need a few hundred watts, so we can manage with solar cells. One advantage of freshwater seas—it wouldn't work on Earth. Your oceans were much too salty—they'd have gobbled up kilowatts and kilowatts."

"Sure you won't change your mind, uncle?" Kumar grinned.

Loren shook his head. Though it had startled him at first, he had now grown quite accustomed to the universal salutation employed by younger Lassans. It was really rather pleasant, suddenly acquiring scores of nieces and nephews.

"No, thanks. I'll stay and watch through the underwater window just in case you get eaten by sharks."

"Sharks!" Kumar said wistfully. "Wonderful, wonderful animals—I wish we had some here. It would make diving much more exciting."

Loren watched with a technician's interest as Brant and Kumar adjusted their gear. Compared with the equipment one needed to wear in space, it was remarkably simple—and the pressure tank was a tiny thing that could easily fit in the palm of one hand.

"That oxygen tank," he said, "I wouldn't have thought it could last more than a couple of minutes."

Brant and Kumar looked at him reproachfully.

"Oxygen!" Brant snorted. "That's a deadly poison at below twenty meters. This bottle holds air—and it's only the emergency supply, good for fifteen minutes."

He pointed to the gill-like structure on the backpack that Kumar was already wearing.

"There's all the oxygen you need dissolved in seawater, if you can extract it. But that takes energy, so you have to have a powercell to run the pumps and filters. I could stay down for a week with this unit if I wanted to."

He tapped the greenly fluorescent computer display on his left wrist.

"This gives all the information I need—depth, powercell status, time to come up, decompression stops—"

Loren risked another foolish question.

"Why are you wearing a facemask, while Kumar isn't?"

"But I am." Kumar grinned. "Look carefully."

"Oh . . . I see. Very neat."

"But a nuisance," Brant said, "unless you practically live in the water, like Kumar. I tried contacts once, and found they hurt my eyes. So I stick to the good old facemask—much less trouble. Ready?"

"Ready, skipper."

They rolled simultaneously over port and starboard sides, their movements so well synchronized that the boat scarcely rocked. Through the thick glass panel set in the keel, Loren watched them glide effortlessly down to the reef. It was, he knew, more than twenty meters down but looked much closer.

Tools and cabling had already been dumped there, and the two divers went swiftly to work repairing the broken grids. Occasionally, they exchanged cryptic monosyllables, but most of the time they worked in complete silence. Each knew his job—and his partner—so well that there was no need for speech.

Time went very swiftly for Loren; he felt he was looking into a new world, as indeed he was. Though he had seen innumerable video records made in the terrestrial oceans, almost all the life that moved below him now was completely unfamiliar. There were whirling discs and pulsating jellies, undulating carpets and corkscrewing spirals—but very few creatures that, by any stretch of the imagination, could be called genuine fish. Just once, near the edge of vision, he caught a glimpse of a swiftly moving torpedo which he was almost sure he recognized. If he was correct, it, too, was an exile from Earth.

He thought that Brant and Kumar had forgotten all about him when he was startled by a message over the underwater intercom.

"Coming up. We'll be with you in twenty minutes. Everything okay?"

"Fine," Loren answered. "Was that a fish from Earth I spotted just now?"

"I never noticed."

"Uncle's right, Brant—a twenty-kilo mutant trout went by five minutes ago. Your welding arc scared it away."

They had now left the seabed and were slowly ascending along the graceful catenary of the anchor line. About five meters below the surface they came to a halt.

"This is the dullest part of every dive," Brant said. "We have to wait here for fifteen minutes. Channel two, please—thanks—but not *quite* so loud . . ."

The music-to-decompress-by had probably been chosen by Kumar; its jittery rhythm hardly seemed appropriate to the peaceful underwater scene. Loren was heartily glad he was not immersed in it and was happy to switch off the player as soon as the two divers started to move upward again.

"That's a good morning's work," Brant said as he scrambled onto the deck. "Voltage and current normal. Now we can go home."

Loren's inexpert aid in helping them out of their equipment was gratefully received. Both men were tired and cold but quickly revived after several cups of the hot, sweet liquid the Lassans called "tea," though it bore little resemblance to any terrestrial drink of that name.

Kumar started the motor and got under way, while Brant scrabbled through the jumble of gear at the bottom of the boat and located a small, brightly colored box.

"No, thanks," Loren said as Brant handed him one of the mildly narcotic tablets. "I don't want to acquire any local habits that won't be easy to break."

He regretted the remark as soon as it was made; it must have been prompted by some perverse impulse of the subconscious—or perhaps by his sense of guilt. But Brant had obviously seen no deeper meaning as he lay back, with his hands clasped under his head, staring up into the cloudless sky.

"You can see *Magellan* in the daytime," Loren said, anxious to change the subject, "if you know exactly where to look. But I've never done it myself."

"Mirissa has—often," Kumar interjected. "And she showed me how. You only have to call Astronet for the transit time and then go out and lie on your back. It's like a bright star, straight overhead, and it doesn't seem to be moving at all. But if you look away for even a second, you've lost it."

Unexpectedly, Kumar throttled back the engine, cruised at low power for a few minutes, then brought the boat to a complete halt. Loren glanced around to get his bearings and was surprised to see that they were now at least a kilometer from Tarna. There was another buoy rocking in the water beside them, bearing a large letter P and carrying a red flag.

"Why have we stopped?" asked Loren.

Kumar chuckled and started emptying a small bucket over the side. Luckily, it had been sealed until now; the contents looked suspiciously like blood but smelled far worse. Loren moved as far away as possible in the limited confines of the boat.

"Just calling on an old friend," Brant said very softly. "Sit still—don't make any noise. She's quite nervous."

She? Loren thought. What's going on?

Nothing whatsoever happened for at least five minutes; Loren would not have believed that Kumar could have remained still for so long. Then he noticed that a dark curved band had appeared, a few meters from the boat, just below the surface of the water. He traced it with his eyes and realized that it formed a ring, completely encircling them.

He also realized, at about the same moment, that Brant and Kumar were not watching it; they were watching *him*. So they're trying to give me a surprise, he told himself; well, we'll see about that . . .

Even so, it took all of Loren's willpower to stifle a cry of sheer terror when what seemed to be a wall of brilliantly— no, *putrescently*—pink flesh emerged from the sea. It rose, dripping, to about half the height of a man and formed an unbroken barrier around them. And as a final horror, its upper surface was almost completely covered with writhing snakes, colored vivid reds and blues.

An enormous tentacle-fringed mouth had risen from the deep and was about to engulf them . . .

Yet clearly they were in no danger; he could tell that from his companions' amused expressions.

"What in God's—Krakan's—name *is* that?" he whispered, trying to keep his voice steady.

"You reacted fine," Brant said admiringly. "Some people hide in the bottom of the boat. It's Polly—for polyp. Pretty Polly. Colonial invertebrate—billions of specialized cells, all cooperating. You had very similar animals on Earth, though I don't believe they were anything like as large."

"I'm sure they weren't," Loren answered fervently. "And if you don't mind me asking—how do we get out of here?"

Brant nodded to Kumar, who brought the engines up to full-power. With astonishing speed for something so huge, the living wall around them sank back into the sea, leaving nothing but an oily ripple on the surface.

"The vibration's scared it," Brant explained. "Look through the viewing glass—now you can see the whole beast."

Below them, something like a tree-trunk ten meters thick was retracting toward the seabed. Now Loren realized that the "snakes" he had seen wriggling on the surface were slender tentacles; back in their normal element, they were waving weightlessly again, searching the waters for what—or whom—they might devour.

"What a monster!" he breathed, relaxing for the first time in many minutes. A warm feeling of pride—even exhilaration—swept over him. He knew that he had passed another test; he had won Brant's and Kumar's approval and accepted it with gratitude.

"Isn't that thing—*dangerous*?" he asked.

"Of course; that's why we have the warning buoy."

87

"Frankly, I'd be tempted to kill it."

"Why?" Brant asked, genuinely shocked. "What harm does it do?"

"Well—surely a creature that size must catch an enormous number of fish."

"Yes, but only Lassan—not fish that *we* can eat. And here's the interesting thing about it. For a long time we wondered how it could persuade fish—even the stupid ones here—to swim into its maw. Eventually, we discovered that it secretes some chemical lure, and that's what started us thinking about electric traps. Which reminds me . . ."

Brant reached for his comset.

"Tarna Three calling Tarna Autorecord—Brant here. We've fixed the grid. Everything functioning normally. No need to acknowledge. End message."

But to everyone's surprise, there was an immediate response from a familiar voice.

"Hello, Brant, Dr. Lorenson. I'm happy to hear that. And I've got some interesting news for you. Like to hear it?"

"Of course, Mayor," Brant answered as the two men exchanged glances of mutual amusement. "Go ahead."

"Central Archives has dug up something surprising. All this has happened before. Two hundred fifty years ago, they tried to build a reef out from North Island by electroprecipitation—a technique that had worked well on Earth. But after a few weeks, the underwater cables were broken—some of them *stolen*. The matter was never followed up because the experiment was a total failure, anyway. Not enough minerals in the water to make it worthwhile. So there you are—you can't blame the Conservers. They weren't around in those days."

Brant's face was such a study in astonishment that Loren burst out laughing.

"And you tried to surprise *me!*" he said. "Well, you certainly proved that there were things in the sea that I'd never imagined.

"But now it looks as if there are some things that *you* never imagined, either."

20. IDYLL

The Tarnans thought it was very funny and pretended not to believe him.

"First you've never been in a boat—now you say you can't ride a bicycle!"

"You should be ashamed of yourself," Mirissa had chided him, with a twinkle in her eye. "The most efficient method of transportation ever invented—and you've never tried it!"

"Not much use in spaceships and too dangerous in cities," Loren had retorted. "Anyway, what is there to learn?" He soon discovered that there was a good deal; biking was not quite as easy as it looked. Though it took real talent actually to fall off the low center-of-gravity, small-wheeled machines (he managed it several times) his initial attempts were frustrating. He would not have persisted without Mirissa's assurance that it was the best way to discover the island—and his own hope that it would also be the best way to discover Mirissa.

The trick, he realized after a few more tumbles, was to ignore the problem completely and leave matters to the body's own reflexes. That was logical enough; if one had to think about every footstep one took, ordinary walking would be impossible. Although Loren accepted this intellectually, it was some time before he could trust his instincts. Once he had overcome that barrier, progress was swift. And at last, as he had hoped, Mirissa offered to show him the remoter byways of the island.

It would have been easy to believe that they were the only two people in the world, yet they could not be more than five kilometers from the village. They had certainly ridden much farther than that, but the narrow cycle track had been designed to take the most picturesque route, which also turned out to be the longest. Although Loren could locate himself in an instant from the position-finder in his comset, he did not bother. It was amusing to pretend to be lost.

Mirissa would have been happier if he had left the comset behind.

"Why must you carry that thing?" she had said, pointing to the control-studded band on his left forearm. "It's nice to get away from people sometimes."

"I agree, but ship's regs are very strict. If Captain Bey wanted me in a hurry and I didn't answer—"

"Well—what would he do? Put you in irons?"

"I'd prefer that to the lecture I'd undoubtedly get. Anyway, I've switched to sleep mode. If Shipcom overrides *that*, it will be a real emergency—and I'd certainly want to be in touch."

Like almost all Terrans for more than a thousand years, Loren would have been far happier without his clothes than without his comset. Earth's history was replete with horror stories of careless or reckless individuals who had died—often within meters of safety—because they could not reach the red EMERGENCY button.

The cycle lane was clearly designed for economy, not heavy traffic. It was less than a meter wide, and at first the inexperienced Loren felt that he was riding along a tightrope. He had to concentrate on Mirissa's back (not an unwelcome task) to avoid falling off. But after the first few kilometers he gained confidence and was able to enjoy the other views, as well. If they met anyone coming in the opposite direction, all parties would have to dismount; the thought of a collision at fifty klicks or more was too horrible to contemplate. It would be a long walk home, carrying their smashed bicycles . . .

Most of the time they rode in perfect silence, broken only when Mirissa pointed out some unusual tree or exceptional beauty spot. The silence itself was something that Loren had never before experienced in his whole life; on Earth he had always been surrounded by sounds—and shipboard life was an entire symphony of reassuring mechanical noises, with occasional heart-stopping alarms.

Here the trees surrounded them with an invisible, anechoic blanket, so that every word seemed sucked into silence the moment it was uttered. At first the sheer novelty of the sensation made it enjoyable, but now Loren was beginning to yearn for something to fill the acoustic vacuum. He was even tempted to summon up a little background music from his comset but felt certain that Mirissa would not approve.

It was a great surprise, therefore, when he heard the beat of some now-familiar Thalassan dance music from the trees ahead. As the narrow road seldom proceeded in a straight line for more than two or three hundred meters, he could not see the source until they rounded a sharp curve and found themselves confronted by a melodious mechanical monster straddling the entire road surface and advancing toward them at a slow walking pace. It looked rather like a robot caterpillar. As they dismounted and let it trundle past, Loren realized that it was an automatic road repairer. He had noticed quite a few rough patches, and even potholes, and had been wondering when the South Island Department of Works would bestir itself to deal with them.

"Why the music?" he asked. "This hardly seems the kind of machine that would appreciate it."

He had barely made his little joke when the robot addressed him severely: "Please do not ride on the road surface within one hundred meters of me, as it is still hardening. Please do not ride on the road surface within one hundred meters of me, as it is still hardening. Thank you."

Mirissa laughed at his surprised expression.

"You're right, of course—it isn't very intelligent. The music is a warning to oncoming traffic."

"Wouldn't some kind of hooter be more effective?"

"Yes, but how—*unfriendly!*"

They pushed their bicycles off the road and waited for the line of articulated tanks, control units, and road-laying mechanisms to move slowly past. Loren could not resist touching the freshly extruded surface; it was warm and slightly yielding and looked moist even though it felt perfectly dry. Within seconds, however, it had become as hard as rock; Loren noted the faint impression of his fingerprint and thought wryly, I've made my mark on Thalassa—until the robot comes this way again.

Now the road was rising up into the hills, and Loren found that unfamiliar muscles in thigh and calf were beginning to call attention to themselves. A little auxiliary power would have been welcomed, but Mirissa had spurned the electric models as too effete. She had not slackened her speed in the least, so Loren had no alternative but to breathe deeply and keep up with her.

What was that faint roar from ahead? Surely no one could be testing rocket engines in the interior of South Island! The sound grew steadily louder as they pedaled onward; Loren identified it only seconds before the source came into view.

By Terran standards, the waterfall was not very impressive—perhaps one hundred meters high and twenty across. A small metal bridge glistening with spray spanned the pool of boiling foam in which it ended.

To Loren's relief, Mirissa dismounted and looked at him rather mischievously.

"Do you notice anything . . . *peculiar?*" she asked, waving toward the scene ahead.

"In what way?" Loren answered, fishing for clues. All he saw was an unbroken vista of trees and vegetation, with the road winding away through it on the other side of the fall.

"The trees—the trees!"

"What about them? I'm not a—botanist."

"Nor am I, but it should be obvious. Just look at them."

He looked, still puzzled. And presently he understood, be-

92

cause a tree is a piece of natural engineering—and he was an engineer.

A different designer had been at work on the other side of the waterfall. Although he could not name any of the trees among which he was standing, they were vaguely familiar, and he was sure that they came from Earth . . . Yes, that was certainly an oak, and somewhere, long ago, he had seen the beautiful yellow flowers on that low bush.

Beyond the bridge, it was a different world. The trees—were they really trees?—seemed crude and unfinished. Some had short, barrel-shaped trunks from which a few prickly branches extended; others resembled huge ferns; others looked like giant, skeletal fingers, with bristly haloes at the joints. And there were no flowers . . .

"*Now* I understand. Thalassa's own vegetation."

"Yes—only a few million years out of the sea. We call this the Great Divide. But it's more like a battlefront between two armies, and no one knows which side will win. Neither, if we can help it! The vegetation from Earth is more advanced; but the natives are better adapted to the chemistry. From time to time one side invades the other—and we move in with shovels before it can get a foothold."

How strange, Loren thought as they pushed their bicycles across the slender bridge. For the first time since landing on Thalassa, I feel that I am indeed on an alien world . . .

These clumsy trees and crude ferns could have been the raw material of the coal beds that had powered the Industrial Revolution—barely in time to save the human race. He could easily believe that a dinosaur might come charging out of the undergrowth at any moment; then he recalled that the terrible lizards had still been a hundred million years in the future, when such plants had flourished on Earth . . .

They were just remounting when Loren exclaimed, "Krakan and damnation!"

"What's the matter?"

Loren collapsed on what, providentially, appeared to be a thick layer of wiry moss.

"Cramp," he muttered through clenched teeth, grabbing at his knotted calf muscles.

"Let me," Mirissa said in a concerned but confident voice.

Under her pleasant, though somewhat amateur, ministrations, the spasms slowly ebbed.

"Thanks," Loren said after a while. "That's much better. But please don't stop."

"Did you really think I would?" she whispered.

And presently, between two worlds, they became one.

IV. KRAKAN

21. ACADEMY

The membership of the Thalassan Academy of Science was strictly limited to the nice round binary number 100000000— or for those who preferred to count on their fingers, 256. *Magellan*'s Science Officer approved of such exclusivity; it maintained standards. And the academy took its responsibilities very seriously; the president had confessed to her that at the moment there were only 241 members, as it had proved impossible to fill all the vacancies with qualified personnel.

Of those 241, no less than 105 were physically present in the academy's auditorium, and 116 had logged in on their comsets. It was a record turnout, and Dr. Anne Varley felt extremely flattered—though she could not suppress a fleeting curiosity about the missing 20.

She also felt a mild discomfort at being introduced as one of Earth's leading astronomers—even though, alas, by the date of *Magellan*'s departure, that had been all too true. Time and Chance had given the late director of the—late—Shklovskiy Lunar Observatory this unique opportunity of survival. She knew perfectly well that she was no more than competent when judged by the standards of such giants as Ackerley or Chandrasekhar or Herschel—still less by those of Galileo or Copernicus or Ptolemy.

"Here it is," she began. "I'm sure you've all seen this map of Sagan Two—the best reconstruction possible from fly-bys and radioholograms. The detail's very poor, of course—ten kilometers at the best—but it's enough to give us the basic facts.

"Diameter—fifteen thousand kilometers, a little larger than

Earth. A dense atmosphere—almost entirely nitrogen. And no oxygen—*fortunately*."

That "fortunately" was always an attention getter; it made the audience sit up with a jolt.

"I understand your surprise; most human beings have a prejudice in favor of breathing. But in the decades before the Exodus, many things happened to change our outlook on the universe.

"The absence of other living creatures—past or present—in the Solar System and the failure of the SETI programs despite sixteen centuries of effort convinced virtually everyone that life must be very rare elsewhere in the universe, and therefore very precious.

"Hence it followed that all life forms were worthy of respect and should be cherished. Some argued that even virulent pathogens and disease vectors should not be exterminated but should be preserved under strict safeguards. 'Reverence for Life' became a very popular phrase during the Last Days—and few applied it exclusively to human life.

"Once the principle of biological noninterference was accepted, certain practical consequences followed. It had long been agreed that we should not attempt any settlement on a planet with intelligent life-forms; the human race had a bad enough record on its home world. Fortunately—or unfortunately!—this situation has never arisen.

"But the argument was taken further. Suppose we found a planet on which animal life had just begun. Should we stand aside and let evolution take its course on the chance that megayears hence intelligence might arise?

"Going still further back—suppose there was only plant life? Only single-cell microbes?

"You may find it surprising that when the very existence of the human race was at stake, men bothered to debate such abstract moral and philosophical questions. But Death focuses the mind on the things that really matter: why are we here, and what should we do?

"The concept of 'Metalaw'—I'm sure you've all heard the term—became very popular. Was it possible to develop legal and moral codes applicable to *all* intelligent creatures, and not merely to the bipedal, air-breathing mammals who had briefly dominated Planet Earth?

"Dr. Kaldor, incidentally, was one of the leaders of the debate. It made him quite unpopular with those who argued that since *H. sapiens* was the only intelligent species known, its survival took precedence over all other considerations. Someone coined the effective slogan, 'If it's Man or Slime Molds, I vote for Man!'

"Fortunately, there's never been a direct confrontation—as far as we know. It may be centuries before we get reports from all the seedships that went out. And if some remain silent—well, the slime molds may have won . . .

"In 3505, during the final session of the World Parliament, certain guidelines—the famous Geneva Directive—were laid down for future planetary colonization. Many thought that they were too idealistic, and there was certainly no way in which they could ever be enforced. But they were an expression of intent—a final gesture of goodwill toward a universe which might never be able to appreciate it.

"Only one of the directive's guidelines concerns us here—but it was the most celebrated and aroused intense controversy, since it ruled out some of the most promising targets.

"The presence of more than a few percent oxygen in a planet's atmosphere is definite proof that life exists there. The element is far too reactive to occur in the free state unless it is continually replenished by plants—or their equivalent. Of course, oxygen doesn't necessarily mean *animal* life, but it sets the stage for it. And even if animal life only rarely leads to intelligence, no other plausible route to it has ever been theorized.

"So, according to the principles of Metalaw, oxygen-bearing planets were placed out of bounds. Frankly, I doubt so drastic a decision would have been made if the quantum drive hadn't given us essentially unlimited range—and power.

"Now let me tell you our plan of operation, when we have reached Sagan Two. As you will see by the map, more than fifty percent of the surface is ice covered, to an estimated average depth of three kilometers. All the oxygen we shall ever need!

"When it's established its final orbit, *Magellan* will use the quantum drive, at a small fraction of full-power, to act as a torch. It will burn off the ice and simultaneously crack the steam into oxygen and hydrogen. The hydrogen will quickly leak away into space; we may help it with tuned lasers, if necessary.

"In only twenty years, Sagan Two will have a ten percent O_2 atmosphere, though it will be too full of nitrogen oxides and other poisons to be breatheable. About that time we'll start dumping specially developed bacteria, and even plants, to accelerate the process. But the planet will still be far too cold; even allowing for the heat we've pumped into it, the temperature will be below freezing everywhere except for a few hours near noon at the Equator.

"So that's where we use the quantum drive, probably for the last time. *Magellan*, which has spent its entire existence in space, will finally descend to the surface of a planet.

"And then, for about fifteen minutes every day at the appropriate time, the drive will be switched on at the maximum power the structure of the ship—and the bedrock on which it is resting—can withstand. We won't know how long the operation will take until we have made the first tests; it may be necessary to move the ship again if the initial site is geologically unstable.

"At a first approximation, it appears that we'll need to operate the drive for thirty years, to slow the planet until it drops sunward far enough to give it a temperate climate. And we'll have to run the drive for another twenty-five years to circularize the orbit. But for much of that time Sagan Two will be quite livable—though the winters will be fierce until final orbit is achieved.

"So then we will have a virgin planet, larger than Earth, with about forty percent ocean and a mean temperature of twenty-five degrees. The atmosphere will have an oxygen content seventy percent of Earth's—but still rising. It will be time to awaken the nine hundred thousand sleepers still in hibernation and present them with a new world.

"That is the scenario unless unexpected developments—or discoveries—force us to depart from it. And if the worst comes to the worst . . . "

Dr. Varley hesitated, then smiled grimly.

"No—whatever happens, you won't be seeing us again! If Sagan Two is impossible, there is another target, thirty light-years farther on. It may be an even better one.

"Perhaps we will eventually colonize both. But that is for the future to decide."

The discussion took a little time to get under way; most of the Academicians seemed stunned, though their applause was certainly genuine. The president, who through long experience always had a few questions prepared in advance, started the ball rolling.

"A trivial point, Dr. Varley—but who or what is Sagan Two named after?"

"A writer of scientific romances, early Third Millennium."

That broke the ice, just as the president had intended.

"You mentioned, Doctor, that Sagan Two has at least one satellite. What will happen to it, when you change the planet's orbit?"

"Nothing, apart from very slight perturbations. It will move along with its primary."

"If the directive of—what was it, 3500—"

"3505"

"—had been ratified earlier, would we be here now? I mean, Thalassa would have been out of bounds!"

101

"It's a very good question, and we've often debated it. The 2751 seeding mission—your Mother Ship on South Island—would certainly have gone against the directive. Luckily, the problem hasn't arisen. Since you have no land animals here, the principle of noninterference hasn't been violated."

"This is very speculative," one of the youngest of the Academicians said—to the obvious amusement of many of her elders. "Granted that oxygen means life, how can you be sure that the reverse proposition is true? One can imagine all sorts of creatures—even intelligent ones—on planets with no oxygen, even with no atmosphere. If our evolutionary successors are intelligent *machines*, as many philosophers have suggested, they'd prefer an atmosphere in which they wouldn't rust. Have you any idea how old Sagan Two is? It might have passed through the oxygen-biological era; there could be a machine civilization waiting for you there."

There were a few groans from dissenters in the audience, and someone muttered "science fiction!" in tones of disgust. Dr. Varley waited for the disturbance to die away, then answered briefly, "We've not lost much sleep over that. And if we did run into a machine civilization, the principle of noninterference would hardly matter. I'd be much more worried about what it would do to *us* than the other way round!"

A very old man—the oldest person Dr. Varley had seen in Thalassa—was slowly rising to his feet at the back of the room. The chairman scribbled a quick note and passed it over: "Prof. Derek Winslade—115—G.O.M. of T. science—historian." Dr. Varley puzzled over G.O.M. for a few seconds before some mysterious flash of insight told her that it stood for "Grand Old Man."

And it would be typical, she thought, if the dean of Lassan science was an historian. In all their seven hundred years of history, the Three Islands had produced only a handful of original thinkers.

Yet this did not necessarily merit criticism. The Lassans had been forced to build up the infrastructure of civilization from zero; there had been little opportunity, or incentive, for any research that was not of direct practical application. And there was a more serious and subtle problem—that of population. At any one time, in any one scientific discipline, there would never be enough workers on Thalassa to reach "critical mass"—the minimum number of reacting minds needed to ignite fundamental research into some new field of knowledge.

Only in mathematics—as in music—were there rare exceptions to this rule. A solitary genius—a Ramanujan or a Mozart—could arise from nowhere and sail strange seas of thought alone. The famous example from Lassan science was Francis Zoltan (214–242); his name was still revered five hundred years later, but Dr. Varley had certain reservations even about his undoubted skills. No one, it seemed to her, had really understood his discoveries in the field of hyper-transfinite numbers; still less extended them further—the true test of all genuine breakthroughs. Even now, his famous "Last Hypothesis" defied either proof or disproof.

She suspected—though she was far too tactful to mention this to her Lassan friends—that Zoltan's tragically early death had exaggerated his reputation, investing his memory with wistful hopes of what might have been. The fact that he had disappeared while swimming off North Island had inspired legions of romantic myths and theories—disappointment in love, jealous rivals, inability to discover critical proofs, terror of the hyperinfinite itself—none of which had the slightest factual foundation. But they had all added to the popular image of Thalassa's greatest genius, cut down in the prime of his achievement.

What was the old professor saying? Oh, dear—there was always someone during the question period who brought up a totally irrelevant subject or seized the opportunity to expound a pet theory. Through long practice, Dr. Varley was quite good at dealing with such interpolators and could usually get a laugh at their expense. But she would have to be polite to a G.O.M., surrounded by respectful colleagues, on his own territory.

"Professor, ah, Winsdale"—'Wins*lade*' the chairman whispered urgently, but she decided that any correction would only make matters worse—"the question you have asked is a very good one but should really be the subject of another lecture. Or series of lectures; even then, it would barely scratch the subject.

"But to deal with your first point. We have heard that criticism several times—it is simply not true. We have made no attempt to keep the 'secret,' as you call it, of the quantum drive. The complete theory is in the ship's Archives and is among the material being transferred to your own.

"Having said that, I don't want to raise any false hopes. Frankly, there is *no one* in the ship's active crew who really understands the drive. We know how to use it—that's all.

"There are three scientists in hibernation who are supposed to be experts on the drive. If we have to wake them up before we reach Sagan Two, we'll be in really serious trouble.

"Men went insane trying to visualize the geometrodynamic structure of superspace, and asking why the universe originally had eleven dimensions instead of a nice number like ten or twelve. When I took the Propulsion Basics course, my instructor said; 'If you could understand the quantum drive, you wouldn't be here—you'd be up on Lagrange One at the Institute for Advanced Studies.' And he gave me a useful comparison that helped me get to sleep again when I had nightmares trying to imagine what ten to the minus thirty three centimeters really means.

"'*Magellan*'s crew only has to know what the drive *does*,' my instructor told me. 'They're like engineers in charge of an electric distribution network. As long as they know how to switch the power around, they don't have to know how it's generated. It may come from something simple, like an oil-fueled dynamo or a solar panel or a water turbine. They would certainly understand the principles behind these—but they wouldn't need to in order to do their jobs perfectly well.

"'Or the electricity might come from something more complex, like a fission reactor or a thermonuclear fusor or a muon catalyzer or a Penrose Node or a Hawking-Schwarzschild kernel—you see what I mean? *Somewhere* along the line they'd have to give up any hope of comprehension; but they'd still be perfectly competent engineers, capable of switching electric power where and when it was needed.'

"In the same way, we can switch *Magellan* from Earth to Thalassa—and, I hope, on to Sagan Two—without really knowing what we're doing. But one day, perhaps centuries hence, we will again be able to match the genius that produced the quantum drive.

"And—who knows?—you may do it first. Some latter-day Francis Zoltan may be born on Thalassa. And then perhaps *you* will come to visit us."

She didn't really believe it. But it was a nice way to end, and it drew a tremendous round of applause.

22. KRAKAN

"We can do it with no trouble, of course," said Captain Bey thoughtfully. "Planning's essentially complete—that vibration problem with the compressors seems to be solved—site preparation is ahead of schedule. There's no doubt that we can spare the men and equipment—but is it really a good idea?" He looked at his five senior officers gathered around the oval table in the Terra Nova staff conference room; with one accord they all looked at Dr. Kaldor, who sighed and spread his hands in resignation.

"So it's not a purely technical problem. Tell me all I have to know."

"This is the situation," Deputy Captain Malina said. The lights dimmed, and the Three Islands covered the table, floating a fraction of a centimeter above it like some beautifully detailed model. But this was no model, for if the scale was expanded enough, one could watch the Lassans going about their business.

"I think the Lassans are still scared of Mount Krakan, though really it's a very well behaved volcano—after all, it's never actually *killed* anyone! And it's the key to the inter-island communications system. The summit is six kilometers above sea level—the highest point on the planet, of course. So it's the ideal site for an antenna park; all long-distance services are routed through here and beamed back to the two other islands."

"It's always seemed a little odd to me," Kaldor said mildly, "that after two thousand years we've not found anything better than radio waves."

106

"The universe came equipped with only one electromagnetic spectrum, Dr. Kaldor—we have to make the best use of it we can. And the Lassans are fortunate; because even the extreme ends of the North and South islands are only three hundred kilometers apart, Mount Krakan can blanket them both. They can manage very nicely without comsats.

"The only problem is accessibility—and weather. The local joke is that Krakan's the only place on the planet that has any. Every few years someone has to climb the mountain, repair a few antennas, replace some solar cells and batteries—and shovel away a lot of snow. No real problem but a lot of hard work."

"Which," interjected Surgeon Commander Newton, "Lassans avoid whenever possible. Not that I blame them for saving their energies for more important things—like sports and athletics."

She could have added "making love," but that was already a sensitive subject with many of her colleagues, and the remark might not be appreciated.

"Why do they have to *climb* the mountain?" Kaldor asked. "Why don't they just fly to the top? They've got vertical-lift aircraft."

"Yes, but the air's thin up there—and what there is tends to be boisterous. After several bad accidents, the Lassans decided to do it the hard way."

"I see," Kaldor said thoughtfully. "It's the old noninterference problem. Will we weaken their self-reliance? Only to a trivial extent, I'd say. And if we *don't* accede to such a modest request, we'd provoke resentment. Justified, too, considering the help they're giving us with the ice plant."

"I feel exactly the same way. Any objections? Very good. Mister Lorenson—please make the arrangements. Use whichever spaceplane you think fit, as long as it's not needed for Operation Snowflake."

Moses Kaldor had always loved mountains; they made him

107

feel nearer to the God whose nonexistence he still sometimes resented.

From the rim of the great caldera, he could look down into a sea of lava, long since congealed but still emitting wisps of smoke from a dozen crevasses. Beyond that, far to the west, both the big islands were clearly visible, lying like dark clouds on the horizon.

The stinging cold and the need to make each breath count added a zest to every moment. Long ago he had come across a phrase in some ancient travel or adventure book: "Air like wine." At the time he had wished he could ask the author just how much wine he'd breathed lately; but now the expression no longer seemed so ridiculous.

"Everything's unloaded, Moses. We're ready to fly back."

"Thank you, Loren. I felt like waiting here until you collect everyone in the evening, but it might be risky to stay too long at this altitude."

"The engineers have brought oxygen bottles, of course."

"I wasn't thinking only of that. My namesake once got into a lot of trouble on a mountain."

"Sorry—I don't understand."

"Never mind; it was a long, long time ago."

As the spaceplane lifted off the rim of the crater, the work party waved cheerfully up at them. Now that all the tools and equipment had been unloaded, they were engaged in the essential preliminary to any Lassan project. Someone was making tea.

Loren was careful to avoid the complex mass of antennas, of practically every known design, as he climbed slowly up into the sky. They were all aimed toward the two islands dimly visible in the west; if he interrupted their multiple beams countless gigabits of information would be irretrievably lost, and the Lassans would be sorry that they ever asked him to help.

"You're not heading toward Tarna?"

"In a minute. I want to look at the mountain first. Ah—there it is!"

"What? Oh, I see. Krakan!"

The borrowed expletive was doubly appropriate. Beneath them, the ground had been split into a deep ravine about a hundred meters wide. And at the bottom of that ravine lay Hell.

The fires from the heart of this young world were still burning here, just below the surface. A glowing river of yellow, flecked with crimson, was moving sluggishly toward the sea. How could they be sure, Kaldor wondered, that the volcano had really settled down and was not merely biding its time?

But the river of lava was not their objective. Beyond it lay a small crater about a kilometer across, on the rim of which stood the stump of a single ruined tower. As they came closer, they could see that there had once been three such towers, equally spaced around the rim of the caldera, but of the other two only the foundations were left.

The floor of the crater was covered with a mass of tangled cables and metal sheets, obviously the remains of the great radio reflector that had once been suspended here. At its center lay the wreckage of the receiving and transmitting equipment, partly submerged in a small lake formed by the frequent rainstorms over the mountain.

They circled the ruins of the last link with Earth, neither caring to intrude on the thoughts of the other. At last Loren broke the silence.

"It's a mess—but it wouldn't be hard to repair. Sagan Two is only twelve degrees north—closer to the Equator than Earth was. Even easier to point the beam there with an offset antenna."

"Excellent idea. When we've finished building our shield, we could help them get started. Not that they should need much help, for there's certainly no hurry. After all, it will be almost four centuries before they can hear from us again—even if we start transmitting just as soon as we arrive."

109

Loren finished recording the scene and prepared to fly down the slope of the mountain before turning toward South Island. He had descended scarcely a thousand meters when Kaldor said in a puzzled voice, "What's that smoke over to the northeast? It looks like a signal."

Halfway to the horizon, a thin white column was rising against the cloudless blue of the Thalassan sky. It had certainly not been there a few minutes before.

"Let's have a look. Perhaps there's a boat in trouble."

"You know what it reminds me of?" Kaldor said.

Loren answered with a silent shrug.

"A spouting whale. When they came up to breathe, the big cetaceans used to blow out a column of water vapor. It looked very much like that."

"There are two things wrong with your interesting theory," Loren said. "That column is now at least a kilometer high. Some whale!"

"Agreed. And whale spouts only lasted a few seconds— this is continuous. What's your second objection?"

"According to the chart, that's not open water. So much for the boat theory."

"But that's ridiculous—Thalassa is *all* ocean—oh, I see. The Great Eastern Prairie. Yes—there's its edge. You'd almost imagine that was land down there."

Coming swiftly toward them was the floating continent of seaborne vegetation that covered much of the Thalassan oceans and generated virtually all the oxygen in the planet's atmosphere. It was one continuous sheet of vivid—almost virulent—green and looked solid enough to walk upon. Only the complete absence of hills or any other change of elevation revealed its true nature.

But in one region, about a kilometer across, the floating prairie was neither flat nor unbroken. Something was boiling beneath the surface, throwing up great clouds of steam and occasional masses of tangled weed.

"I should have remembered," Kaldor said. "Child of Krakan."

"Of course," Loren answered. "That's the first time it's been active since we arrived. So this is how the other islands were born."

"Yes—the volcanic plume is moving steadily eastward. Perhaps in a few thousand years the Lassans will have a whole archipelago."

They circled for another few minutes, then turned back toward East Island. To most spectators, this submarine volcano, still struggling to be born, would have been an awesome sight.

But not to men who had seen the destruction of a Solar System.

23. ICE DAY

The presidential yacht, *alias* Inter-Island Ferry Number One, had certainly never looked so handsome at any previous stage of its three-centuries-long career. Not only was it festooned with bunting, but it had been given a new coat of white paint. Unfortunately, either paint or labor had become exhausted before the job was quite finished, so the captain had to be careful to anchor with only the starboard side visible from land.

President Farradine was also ceremonially attired in a striking outfit (designed by Mrs. President) that made him look like a cross between a Roman emperor and a pioneer astronaut. He did not appear altogether at ease in it; Capt. Sirdar Bey was glad that *his* uniform consisted of the plain white shorts, open-neck shirt, shoulder badges, and gold-braided cap in which he felt completely at home—though it was hard to remember when he had last worn it.

Despite the president's tendency to trip over his toga, the official tour had gone very well, and the beautiful onboard model of the freezing plant had worked perfectly. It had produced an unlimited supply of hexagonal ice wafers just the right size to fit into a tumbler of cool drink. But the visitors could hardly be blamed for failing to understand the appropriateness of the name Snowflake; after all, few on Thalassa had ever seen snow.

And now they had left the model behind to inspect the real thing, which covered several hectares of the Tarna coastline. It had taken some time to shuttle the president and his entourage, Captain Bey and his officers, and all the other guests from yacht to shore. Now, in the last light of day, they were standing respectfully around the rim of a hexagonal block of ice twenty meters across and two meters thick. Not only was it the largest mass of frozen water that anyone had ever seen— it was probably the largest on the planet. Even at the Poles, ice seldom had a chance to form. With no major continents to block circulation, the rapidly moving currents from the equatorial regions quickly melted any incipient floes.

"But why is it *that* shape?" the president asked.

Deputy Captain Malina sighed; he was quite sure that this had already been explained several times.

"It's the old problem of covering any surface with identical tiles," he said patiently. "You have only three choices— squares, triangles, or hexagons. In our case, the hex is slightly more efficient and easier to handle. The blocks—over two hundred of them, each weighing six hundred tons—will be keyed into each other to build up the shield. It will be a kind of ice-sandwich three layers thick. When we accelerate, all the blocks will fuse together to make a single huge disk. Or a blunt cone, to be precise."

"You've given me an idea." The president was showing more animation than he had done all afternoon. "We've never had ice-skating on Thalassa. It was a beautiful sport—and there was a game called ice-hockey, though I'm not sure I'd like to revive *that*, from the vids I've seen of it. But it would be wonderful if you could make us an ice-rink in time for the Olympics. Would that be possible?"

"I'll have to think about it," Deputy Captain Malina replied rather faintly. "It's a very interesting idea. Perhaps you'll let me know how much ice you'd need."

"I'll be delighted. And it will be an excellent way of using all this freezing plant when it's done its job."

A sudden explosion saved Malina the necessity of a reply. The fireworks had started, and for the next twenty minutes the sky above the island erupted with polychromatic incandescence.

113

The Lassans loved fireworks and indulged in them at every opportunity. The display was intermingled with laser imagery—even more spectacular, and considerably safer, but lacking the smell of gunpowder that added that final touch of magic.

When all the festivities were over and the VIPs had departed to the ship, Captain Malina said thoughtfully, "The president's full of surprises, even though he does have a one-track mind. I'm tired of hearing about his damned Olympics—but that ice-rink is an excellent idea and should generate a lot of goodwill for us."

"I've won my bet, though," Lieutenant Commander Lorenson said.

"What bet was that?" Captain Bey asked.

Malina gave a laugh.

"I would never have believed it. Sometimes the Lassans don't seem to have any *curiosity*—they take everything for granted. Though I suppose we should be flattered that they have such faith in our technological know-how. Perhaps they think we have antigravity!

"It was Loren's idea that I should leave it out of the briefing—and he was right. President Farradine never bothered to ask what would have been *my* very first question— just how we're going to lift a hundred and fifty thousand tons of ice up to *Magellan*."

24. ARCHIVE

Moses Kaldor was happy to be left alone, for as many hours or days as he could be spared, in the cathedral calm of First Landing. He felt like a young student again, confronted with all the art and knowledge of mankind. The experience was both exhilarating and depressing; a whole universe lay at his fingertips, but the fraction of it he could explore in an entire lifetime was so negligible that he was sometimes almost overwhelmed with despair. He was like a hungry man presented with a banquet that stretched as far as the eye could see—a feast so staggering that it completely destroyed his appetite.

And yet all this wealth of wisdom and culture was only a tiny fraction of mankind's heritage. Much that Moses Kaldor knew and loved was missing—not, he was well aware, by accident but by deliberate design.

A thousand years ago, men of genius and goodwill had rewritten history and gone through the libraries of Earth deciding what should be saved and what should be abandoned to the flames. The criterion of choice was simple, though often very hard to apply. Only if it would contribute to survival and social stability on the new worlds would any work of literature, any record of the past, be loaded into the memory of the seedships.

The task was, of course, impossible as well as heartbreaking. With tears in their eyes, the selection panels had thrown away the Veda, the Bible, the Tripitaka, the Qur'an, and all the immense body of literature—fiction and nonfiction—that was based upon them. Despite all the wealth of beauty and wisdom these works contained, they could not be allowed to

115

reinfect virgin planets with the ancient poisons of religious hatred, belief in the supernatural, and the pious gibberish with which countless billions of men and women had once comforted themselves at the cost of addling their minds.

Lost also in the great purge were virtually all the works of the supreme novelists, poets, and playwrights, which would in any case have been meaningless without their philosophical and cultural background. Homer, Shakespeare, Milton, Tolstoy, Melville, Proust—the last great fiction writer before the electronic revolution overwhelmed the printed page—all that was left were a few hundred thousand carefully selected passages. Excluded were everything that concerned war, crime, violence, and the destructive passions. If the newly designed—and it was hoped improved—successors to *H. sapiens* rediscovered these, they would doubtless create their own literature in response. There was no need to give them premature encouragement.

Music—except for opera—had fared better, as had the visual arts. Nevertheless, the sheer volume of material was so overwhelming that selection had been imperative, though sometimes arbitrary. Future generations on many worlds would wonder about Mozart's first thirty-eight symphonies, Beethoven's Second and Fourth, and Sibelius's Third to Sixth.

Moses Kaldor was deeply aware of his responsibility and also conscious of his inadequacy—of *any* one man's inadequacy, however talented he might be—to handle the task that confronted him. Up there aboard *Magellan*, safely stored in its gigantic memory banks, was much that the people of Thalassa had never known and certainly much that they would greedily accept and enjoy, even if they did not wholly understand. The superb twenty-fifth century recreation of the *Odyssey*, the war classics that looked back in anguish across half a millennium of peace, the great Shakspearean tragedies in Feinberg's miraculous Lingua translation, Lee Chow's *War and Peace*—it would take hours and days even to name all the possibilities.

Sometimes, as he sat in the library of the First Landing Complex, Kaldor was tempted to play god with these reasonably happy and far-from-innocent people. He would compare the listings from the memory banks here with those aboard the ship, noting what had been expunged or condensed. Even though he disagreed in principle with any form of censorship, often he had to admit the wisdom of the deletions—at least in the days when the colony was founded. But now that it was successfully established, perhaps a little disturbance, or injection of creativity, might be in order . . .

Occasionally, he was disturbed himself either by calls from the ship or by parties of young Lassans being given guided tours back to the beginning of their history. He did not mind the interruptions, and there was one that he positively welcomed.

Most afternoons, except when what passed for urgent business in Tarna prevented her, Mirissa would come riding up the hill on her beautiful palomino gelding, Bobby. The visitors had been much surprised to find horses on Thalassa, since they had never seen any alive on Earth. But the Lassans loved animals and had recreated many from the vast files of genetic material they had inherited. Sometimes they were quite useless—or even a nuisance, like the engaging little squirrel monkeys that were always stealing small objects from Tarnan households.

Mirissa would invariably bring some delicacy—usually fruit or one of the many local cheeses—which Kaldor would accept with gratitude. But he was even more grateful for her company; who would believe that often he had addressed five million people—more than half the last generation!—yet was now content with an audience of one . . .

"Because you've descended from a long line of librarians," Moses Kaldor said, "you only think in megabytes. But may I remind you that the name 'library' comes from a word meaning *book*. Do you have books on Thalassa?"

"Of course we do," Mirissa said indignantly; she had not

117

yet learned to tell when Kaldor was joking. "Millions . . . well, thousands. There's a man on North Island who prints about ten a year, in editions of a few hundred. They're beautiful—and very expensive. They all go as gifts for special occasions. I had one on my twenty-first birthday—*Alice in Wonderland.*"

"I'd like to see it someday. I've always loved books and have almost a hundred on the ship. Perhaps that's why whenever I hear someone talking bytes, I divide mentally by a million and think of one book . . . one gigabyte equals a thousand books, and so on. That's the only way I can grasp what's really involved when people talk about data banks and information transfer. Now, how big is your library?"

Without taking her eyes off Kaldor, Mirissa let her fingers wander over the keyboard of her console.

"That's another thing I've never been able to do," he said admiringly. "Someone once said that after the twenty-first century, the human race divided into two species—Verbals and Digitals. I *can* use a keyboard when I have to, of course—but I prefer to talk to my electronic colleagues."

"As of the last hourly check," Mirissa said, "six hundred and forty-five terabytes."

"Umm—almost a billion books. And what was the initial size of the library?"

"I can tell you that without looking it up. Six hundred and forty."

"So in seven hundred years—"

"Yes, yes—we've managed to produce only a few million books."

"I'm not criticizing; after all, quality is far more important than quantity. I'd like you to show me what you consider the best works of Lassan literature—music, too. The problem *we* have to decide is what to give you. *Magellan* has over a thousand megabooks aboard, in the General Access bank. Do you realize just what that implies?"

"If I said yes, it would stop you from telling me. I'm not that cruel."

"Thank you, my dear. Seriously, it's a terrifying problem that's haunted me for years. Sometimes I think that the Earth was destroyed none too soon; the human race was being crushed by the information it was generating.

"At the end of the Second Millennium, it was producing only—only!—the equivalent of a million books a year. And I'm referring merely to information that was presumed to be of some permanent value, so it was stored indefinitely.

"By the Third Millennium, the figure had multiplied by at least a hundred. Since writing was invented, until the end of Earth, it's been estimated that ten thousand million books were produced. And as I told you, we have about ten percent of that on board.

"If we dumped it all on you, even assuming you have the storage capacity, you'd be overwhelmed. It would be no kindness—it would totally inhibit your cultural and scientific growth. And most of the material would mean nothing at all to you; you'd take centuries to sort the wheat from the chaff . . ."

Strange, Kaldor said to himself, that I've not thought of the analogy before. This is precisely the danger that the opponents of SETI kept raising. Well, we never communicated with extraterrestrial intelligence, or even detected it. But the Lassans have done just that—and the ETs are *us* . . .

Yet despite their totally different backgrounds, he and Mirissa had so much in common. Her curiosity and intelligence were traits to be encouraged; not even among his fellow crewmembers was there anyone with whom he could have such stimulating conversations. Sometimes Kaldor was so hard put to answer her questions that the only defense was a counterattack.

"I'm surprised," he told her after a particularly thorough cross-examination on Solar politics, "that you never took over from your father and worked here full-time. This would be the perfect job for you."

"I was tempted. But he spent all his life answering other

119

people's questions and assembling files for the bureaucrats on North Island. He never had time to do anything himself."

"And you?"

"I like collecting facts, but I also like to see them used. That's why they made me deputy director of the Tarna Development Project."

"Which I fear may have been slightly sabotaged by our operations. Or so the director told me when I met him coming out of the mayor's office."

"You know Brant wasn't serious. It's a long-range plan, with only approximate completion dates. If the Olympic Ice Stadium *is* built here, then the project may have to be modified—for the better, most of us believe. Of course, the Northers want to have it on their side—they think that First Landing is quite enough for us."

Kaldor chuckled; he knew all about the generations-old rivalry between the two islands.

"Well—isn't it? Especially now that you have us as an additional attraction. You mustn't be too greedy."

They had grown to know—and like—each other so well that they could joke about Thalassa or *Magellan* with equal impartiality. And there were no longer any secrets between them; they could talk frankly about Loren and Brant, and at last Moses Kaldor found he could speak of Earth.

". . . Oh, I've lost count of my various jobs, Mirissa—most of them weren't very important, anyway. The one I held longest was professor of political science in Cambridge, Mars. And you can't imagine the confusion *that* caused, because there was an older university at a place called Cambridge, *Mass.*—and a still older one in Cambridge, England.

"But toward the end, Evelyn and I got more and more involved in the immediate social problems, and the planning for the Final Exodus. It seemed that I had some—well, oratorical talent—and could help people face what future was left to them.

"Yet we never *really* believed that the End would be in our time—who could! And if anyone had ever told me that I should leave Earth and everything I loved . . ."

A spasm of emotion crossed his face, and Mirissa waited in sympathetic silence until he had regained his composure. There were so many questions she wanted to ask that it might take a lifetime to answer them all; and she had only a year before *Magellan* set forth once more for the stars.

"When they told me I was needed, I used all my philo- sophical and debating skills to prove them wrong. I was too old; all the knowledge I had was stored in the memory banks; other men could do a better job . . . everything except the *real* reason.

"In the end, Evelyn made up my mind for me; it's true, Mirissa, that in some ways women are much stronger than men—but why am I telling *you* that?

"'They need you,' her last message said. 'We have spent forty years together—now there is only a month left. Go with my love. Do not try to find me.'

"I shall never know if she saw the end of the Earth as I did—when we were leaving the Solar System."

25. SCORP

He had seen Brant stripped before, when they had gone on that memorable boat-ride, but had never realized how formidably muscled the younger man was. Though Loren had always taken good care of his body, there had been little opportunity for sport or exercise since leaving Earth. Brant, however, was probably involved in some heavy physical exertion every day of his life—and it showed. Loren would have absolutely no chance against him unless he could conjure up one of the reputed martial arts of old Earth—none of which he had ever known.

The whole thing was perfectly ridiculous. There were his fellow officers grinning their stupid heads off. There was Captain Bey holding a stopwatch. And there was Mirissa with an expression that could only be described as smug.

". . . two . . . one . . . zero . . . GO!" the captain said. Brant moved like a striking cobra. Loren tried to avoid the onslaught but discovered to his horror that he had no control over his body. Time seemed to have slowed down . . . His legs were made of lead and refused to obey him . . . He was about to lose not only Mirissa but his very manhood . . .

At that point, luckily, he had woken up, but the dream still bothered him. Its sources were obvious, but that did not make it any the less disturbing. He wondered if he should tell it to Mirissa.

Certainly he could never tell it to Brant, who was still perfectly friendly but whose company he now found embarrassing. Today, however, he positively welcomed it; if he was right, they were now confronted with something very much greater than their own private affairs.

He could hardly wait to see the reaction when Brant met the unexpected visitor who had arrived during the night.

The concrete-lined channel that brought seawater into the freezing plant was a hundred meters long and ended in a circular pool holding just enough water for one snowflake. Since pure ice was an indifferent building material, it was necessary to strengthen it, and the long strands of kelp from the Great Eastern Prairie made a cheap and convenient reinforcement. The frozen composite had been nicknamed icecrete and was guaranteed not to flow, glacierlike, during the weeks and months of *Magellan*'s acceleration.

"There it is."

Loren stood with Brant Falconer at the edge of the pool, looking down through a break in the matted raft of marine vegetation. The creature eating the kelp was built on the same general plan as a terrestrial lobster—but was more than twice the size of a man.

"Have you ever seen anything like *that* before?"

"No," Brant answered fervently, "and I'm not at all sorry. What a monster! How did you catch it?"

"We didn't. It swam—or crawled—in from the sea, along the channel. Then it found the kelp and decided to have a free lunch."

"No wonder it has pinchers like that; those stems are really tough."

"Well, at least it's a vegetarian."

"I'm not sure I'd care to put that to the test."

"I was hoping you could tell us something about it."

"We don't know a hundredth of the creatures in the Lassan sea. One day we'll build some research subs and go into deep water. But there are so many other priorities, and not enough people are interested."

They soon will be, Lorenson thought grimly. Let's see how long Brant takes to notice for himself. . . .

"Science Officer Varley has been checking the records. She tells me that there was something very much like this on Earth millions of years ago. The paleontologists gave it a good name—sea scorpion. Those ancient oceans must have been exciting places."

"Just the sort of thing Kumar would like to chase," Brant said. "What are you going to do with it?"

"Study it and then let it go."

"I see you've already tagged it."

So Brant's noticed, thought Loren. Good for him.

"No—we haven't. Look more carefully."

There was a puzzled expression on Brant's face as he knelt at the side of the tank. The giant scorpion ignored him completely as it continued to snip away at the seaweed with its formidable pinchers.

One of those pinchers was not altogether as nature had designed it. At the hinge of the right-hand claw there was a loop of wire twisted around several times like a crude bracelet.

Brant recognized that wire. His jaw dropped, and for a moment he was at a loss for words.

"So I guessed right," Lorenson said. "Now you know what happened to your fish-trap. I think we'd better talk to Dr. Varley again—not to mention your own scientists."

"I'm an astronomer," Anne Varley had protested from her office aboard *Magellan*. "What you need is a combination of zoologist, paleontologist, ethologist—not to mention a few other disciplines. But I've done my best to set up a search program, and you'll find the result dumped in your bank two under file heading SCORP. Now all you need to do is to search *that*—and good luck to you."

Despite her disclaimer, Dr. Varley had done her usual efficient job of winnowing through the almost-infinite store of knowledge in the ship's main memory banks. A pattern was beginning to emerge; meanwhile, the source of all the attention still browsed peacefully in its tank, taking no notice of the continual flow of visitors who came to study or merely to gape.

Despite its terrifying appearance—those pinchers were almost half a meter long and looked capable of taking off a man's head with one neat snip—the creature seemed completely nonaggressive. It made no effort to escape, perhaps because it had found such an abundant source of food. Indeed, it was generally believed that some trace chemical from the kelp had been responsible for luring it here.

If it was able to swim, it showed no inclination to do so, but was content to crawl around on its six stubby legs. Its four-meter-long body was encased in a vividly colored exoskeleton, articulated to give it surprising flexibility.

Another remarkable feature was the fringe of palps, or small tentacles, surrounding the beaklike mouth. They bore a striking—indeed, uncomfortable—resemblance to stubby human fingers and seemed equally dexterous. Although handling food appeared to be their main function, they were clearly capable of much more, and it was fascinating to watch the way that the scorp used them in conjunction with its claws.

Its two sets of eyes—one pair large, and apparently intended for low light, since during the daytime they were kept closed—must also provide it with excellent vision. Altogether, it was superbly equipped to survey and to manipulate its environment—the prime requirements for intelligence.

Yet no one would have suspected intelligence in such a bizarre creature if not for the wire twisted purposefully around its right claw. That, however, proved nothing. As the records showed, there had been animals on Earth who collected foreign objects—often man-made—and used them in extraordinary ways.

If it had not been fully documented, no one would have believed the Australian bowerbird's, or the North American pack rat's, mania for collecting shiny or colored objects, and even arranging them in artistic displays. Earth had been full of such mysteries, which now would never be solved. Perhaps the Thalassan scorp was merely following the same mindless tradition, and for equally inscrutable reasons.

There were several theories. The most popular—because it put the least demands on the scorp's mentality—was that the wire bracelet was merely an ornament. Fixing it in place must have required some dexterity, and there was a good deal of debate as to whether the creature could have done it without assistance.

That assistance, of course, could have been human. Perhaps the scorp was some eccentric scientist's escaped pet, but this seemed very improbable. Since everyone on Thalassa knew everyone else, such a secret could not have been kept for long.

There was one other theory, the most farfetched of all—yet the most thought provoking.

Perhaps the bracelet was a badge of rank.

26. SNOWFLAKE RISING

It was highly skilled work with long periods of boredom, which gave Lt. Owen Fletcher plenty of time to think. Far too much time, in fact.

He was an angler, reeling in a six-hundred-ton catch on a line of almost unimaginable strength. Once a day the self-guided, captive probe would dive down toward Thalassa, spinning out the cable behind it along a complex, thirty-thousand-kilometer curve. It would home automatically on the waiting payload, and when all the checks had been completed, the hoisting would begin.

The critical moments were at lift-off, when the snowflake was snatched out of the freezing plant, and the final approach to *Magellan*, when the huge hexagon of ice had to be brought to rest only a kilometer from the ship. Lifting began at midnight, and from Tarna to the stationary orbit in which *Magellan* was hovering, took just under six hours.

As *Magellan* was in daylight during the rendezvous and assembly, the first priority was keeping the snowflake in shadow, lest the fierce rays of Thalassa's sun boil off the precious cargo into space. Once it was safely behind the big radiation shield, the claws of the robot teleoperators could rip away the insulating foil that had protected the ice during its ascent to orbit.

Next the lifting cradle had to be removed, to be sent back for another load. Sometimes the huge metal plate, shaped like a hexagonal saucepan lid designed by some eccentric cook, stuck to the ice, and a little carefully regulated heating was required to detach it.

At last, the geometrically perfect ice floe would be poised motionless a hundred meters away from *Magellan,* and the really tricky part would begin. The combination of six hundred tons of mass with zero weight was utterly outside the range of human instinctive reaction; only computers could tell what thrusts were needed, in what direction, at what moments of time, to key the artifical iceberg into position. But there was always the possibility of some emergency or unexpected problem beyond the capabilities of even the most intelligent robot; although Fletcher had not yet had to intervene, he would be ready if the time came.

I'm helping to build, he told himself, a giant honeycomb of ice. The first layer of the comb was now almost completed, and there were two more to go. Barring accidents, the shield would be finished in another hundred and fifty days. It would be tested under low acceleration to make sure that all the blocks had fused together properly; and then *Magellan* would set forth upon the final leg of its journey to the stars.

Fletcher was still doing his job conscientiously—but with his mind, not with his heart. That was already lost to Thalassa.

He had been born on Mars, and this world had everything his own barren planet had lacked. He had seen the labor of generations of his ancestors dissolve in flame; why start again centuries from now on yet another world—when Paradise was here?

And, of course, a girl was waiting for him, down there on South Island . . .

He had almost decided that when the time came, he would jump ship. The Terrans could go on without him to deploy their strength and skills—and perhaps break their hearts and bodies—against the stubborn rocks of Sagan Two. He wished them luck; when he had done his duty, his home was here.

Thirty thousand kilometers below, Brant Falconer had also made a crucial decision.

"I'm going to North Island."

Mirissa lay silent; then, after what seemed to Brant a very long time, she said, "Why?" There was no surprise, no regret in her voice; so much, he thought, has changed.

But before he could answer, she added, "You don't like it there."

"Perhaps it is better than here—as things are now. This is no longer my home."

"It will always be your home."

"Not while *Magellan* is still in orbit."

Mirissa reached out her hand in the darkness to the stranger beside her. At least he did not move away.

"Brant," she said, "I never intended this. And nor, I'm quite certain, did Loren."

"That doesn't help much, does it? Frankly, I can't understand what you see in him."

Mirissa almost smiled. How many men, she wondered, had said that to how many women in the course of human history? And how many women had said, "What can you see in *her*?"

There was no way of answering, of course; even the attempt would only make matters worse. But sometimes she had tried, for her own satisfaction, to pinpoint what had drawn her and Loren together since the very moment they had first set eyes upon each other.

The major part was the mysterious chemistry of love, beyond rational analysis, inexplicable to anyone who did not share the same illusion. But there were other elements that could be clearly identified and explained in logical terms. It was useful to know what they were; one day (all too soon!) that wisdom might help her face the moment of parting.

First there was the tragic glamour that surrounded all the Terrans; she did not discount the importance of that, but Loren shared it with all his comrades. What did he have that was so special and that she could not find in Brant?

As lovers, there was little to choose between them; perhaps Loren was more imaginative, Brant more passionate—though had he not become a little perfunctory in the last few weeks?

129

She would be perfectly happy with either. No, it was not *that* . . .

Perhaps she was searching for an ingredient that did not even exist. There was no single element but an entire constellation of qualities. Her instincts, below the level of conscious thought, had added up the score; and Loren had come out a few points ahead of Brant. It could be as simple as that.

There was certainly one respect in which Loren far eclipsed Brant. He had drive, ambition—the very things that were so rare on Thalassa. Doubtless he had been chosen for these qualities; he would need them in the centuries to come.

Brant had no ambition whatsoever, though he was not lacking in enterprise; his still-uncompleted fish-trapping project was proof of that. All he asked from the universe was that it provided him with interesting machines to play with; Mirissa sometimes thought that he included her in that category.

Loren, by contrast, was in the tradition of the great explorers and adventurers. He would help to make history, not merely submit to its imperatives. And yet he could—not often enough but more and more frequently—be warm and human. Even as he froze the seas of Thalassa, his own heart was beginning to thaw.

"What are you going to do on North Island?" Mirissa whispered. Already, they had taken his decision for granted.

"They want me there to help fit out *Calypso*. The Northers don't really understand the sea."

Mirissa felt relieved; Brant was not simply running away—he had work to do.

Work that would help him to forget—until, perhaps, the time came to remember once again.

27. MIRROR OF THE PAST

Moses Kaldor held the module up to the light, peering into it as if he could read its contents.

"It will always seem a miracle to me," he said, "that I can hold a million books between my thumb and forefinger. I wonder what Caxton and Gutenberg would have thought."

"Who?" Mirissa asked.

"The men who started the human race reading. But there's a price we have to pay now for our ingenuity. Sometimes I have a little nightmare and imagine that one of these modules contains some piece of absolutely vital information—say the cure for a raging epidemic—but the address has been lost. It's on *one* of those billion pages, but we don't know which. How frustrating to hold the answer in the palm of your hand and not be able to find it!"

"I don't see the problem," the captain's secretary said. As an expert on information storage and retrieval, Joan LeRoy had been helping with the transfers between Thalassa Archives and the ship. "You'll know the key words; all you have to do is set up a search program. Even a billion pages could be checked in a few seconds."

"You've spoiled my nightmare." Kaldor sighed. Then he brightened. "But often you even don't know the key words. How many times have you come across something that you didn't know you needed—until you found it?"

"Then you're badly organized," said Lieutenant LeRoy.

They enjoyed these little tongue-in-cheek exchanges, and Mirissa was not always sure when to take them seriously. Joan and Moses did not deliberately try to exclude her from their conversations, but their worlds of experience were so utterly different from hers that she sometimes felt that she was listening to a dialogue in an unknown language.

"Anyway, that completes the Master Index. We each know what the other has; now we merely—*merely!*—have to decide what we'd like to transfer. It may be inconvenient, not to say expensive, when we're seventy-five lights apart."

"Which reminds me," Mirissa said. "I don't suppose I should tell you—but there was a delegation from North Island here last week. The president of the science academy, and a couple of physicists."

"Let me guess. The quantum drive."

"Right."

"How did they react?"

"They seemed pleased—and surprised—that it really *was* there. They made a copy, of course."

"Good luck to them; they'll need it. And you might tell them this. Someone once said that the QD's real purpose is nothing as trivial as the exploration of the universe. We'll need its energies one day to stop the cosmos' collapsing back into the primordial black hole—and to start the next cycle of existence."

There was an awed silence; then Joan LeRoy broke the spell.

"Not in the lifetime of *this* administration. Let's get back to work. We still have megabytes to go before we sleep."

It was not all work, and there were times when Kaldor simply had to get away from the library section of First Landing in order to relax. Then he would stroll across to the art gallery, take the computer-guided tour through the Mother Ship (never the same route twice—he tried to cover as much ground as possible) or let the museum carry him back in time.

There was always a long line of visitors—mostly students, or children with their parents—for the Terrama displays. Sometimes Moses Kaldor felt a little guilty at using his privileged status to jump to the head of the queue. He consoled himself with the thought that the Lassans had a whole lifetime in which they could enjoy these panoramas of the world they had never known; he had only months in which to revisit his lost home.

He found it very difficult to convince his new friends that Moses Kaldor had never been in the scenes they sometimes watched together. Everything they saw was at least eight hundred years in his own past, for the Mother Ship had left Earth in 2751—and he had been born in 3541. Yet occasionally there would be a shock of recognition, and some memory would come flooding back with almost unbearable power.

The "Sidewalk Cafe" presentation was the most uncanny and the most evocative. He would be sitting at a small table, under an awning, drinking wine or coffee while the life of a city flowed past him. As long as he did not get up from the table, there was absolutely no way in which his senses could distinguish the display from reality.

In microcosm, the great cities of Earth were brought back to life. Rome, Paris, London, New York—in summer and winter, by night and day, he watched the tourists and business-men and students and lovers go about their ways. Often, realizing that they were being recorded, they would smile at him across the centuries, and it was impossible not to respond.

Other panoramas showed no human beings at all, or even any of the productions of Man. Moses Kaldor looked again, as he had done in that other life, upon the descending smoke of Victoria Falls, the Moon rising above the Grand Canyon, the Himalayan snows, the ice cliffs of Antarctica. Unlike the glimpses of the cities, these things had not changed in the thousand years since they were recorded. And though they had existed long before Man, they had not outlasted him.

28. THE SUNKEN FOREST

The scorp did not seem to be in a hurry; it took a leisurely ten days to travel fifty kilometers. One curious fact was quickly revealed by the sonar beacon that had been attached, not without difficulty, to the angry subject's carapace. The path it traced along the seabed was perfectly straight, as if it knew precisely where it was going.

Whatever its destination might be, it seemed to have found it, at a depth of two hundred and fifty meters. Thereafter, it still kept moving around, but inside a very limited area. This continued for two more days; then the signals from the ultrasonic pinger suddenly stopped in mid-pulse.

That the scorp had been eaten by something even bigger and nastier than itself was far too naive an explanation. The pinger was enclosed in a tough metal cylinder; any conceivable arrangement of teeth, claws, or tentacles would take minutes—at the very least—to demolish it, and it would continue to function quite happily inside any creature that swallowed it whole.

This left only two possibilities, and the first was indignantly denied by the staff of the North Island Underwater Lab.

"*Every* single component had a backup," the director said. "What's more, there was a diagnostic pulse only two seconds earlier; everything was normal. So it could *not* have been an equipment failure."

That left only the impossible explanation. The pinger had been switched off. And to do that, a locking-bar had to be removed.

It could not happen by accident; only by curious meddling—or deliberate intent.

The twenty meter twin-hull *Calypso* was not merely the largest but the only oceanographic research vessel on Thalassa. It was normally based on North Island, and Loren was amused to note the good-natured banter between its scientific crew and their Tarnan passengers, whom they pretended to treat as ignorant fishermen. For their part, the South Islanders lost no opportunity of boasting to the Northers that *they* were the ones who had discovered the scorps. Loren did not remind them that this was not strictly in accord with the facts.

It was a slight shock to meet Brant again, though Loren should have expected it, since the other had been partly responsible for *Calypso*'s new equipment. They greeted each other with cool politeness, ignoring the curious or amused glances of the other passengers. There were few secrets on Thalassa; by this time everyone would know who was occupying the main guest-room of the Leonidas home.

The small underwater sledge sitting on the afterdeck would have been familiar to almost any oceanographer of the last two thousand years. Its metal framework carried three television cameras, a wire basket to hold samples collected by the remote-controlled arm, and an arrangement of water-jets that permitted movement in any direction. Once it had been lowered over the side, the robot explorer could send its images and information back through a fiber-optic cable not much thicker than the lead of a pencil. The technology was centuries old—and still perfectly adequate.

Now the shoreline had finally disappeared, and for the first time Loren found himself completely surrounded by water. He recalled his anxiety on that earlier trip with Brant and Kumar when they had traveled hardly a kilometer from the beach. This time, he was pleased to discover, he felt slightly more at ease despite the presence of his rival. Perhaps it was because he was on a much larger boat . . .

135

"That's odd," Brant said, "I've never seen kelp this far to the west."

At first Loren could see nothing; then he noticed the dark stain low in the water ahead. A few minutes later, the boat was nosing its way through a loose mass of floating vegetation, and the captain slowed speed to a crawl.

"We're almost there, anyway," he said. "No point in clogging our intakes with this stuff. Agreed, Brant?"

Brant adjusted the cursor on the display screen and took a reading.

"Yes—we're only fifty meters from where we lost the pinger. Depth two hundred and ten. Let's get the fish overboard."

"Just a minute," one of the Norther scientists said. "We spent a lot of time and money on that machine, and it's the only one in the world. Suppose it gets tangled up in that damned kelp?"

There was a thoughtful silence; then Kumar, who had been uncharacteristically quiet—perhaps overawed by the high-powered talent from North Island—put in a diffident word.

"It looks much worse from here. Ten meters down, there are almost no leaves—only the big stems, with plenty of room between them. It's like a forest."

Yes, thought Loren, a submarine forest, with fish swimming between the slender, sinuous trunks. While the other scientists were watching the main video screen and the multiple displays of instrumentation, he had put on a set of full-vision goggles, excluding everything from his field of view except the scene ahead of the slowly descending robot. Psychologically, he was no longer on the deck of *Calypso*; the voices of his companions seemed to come from another world that had nothing to do with him.

He was an explorer entering an alien universe, not knowing what he might encounter. It was a restricted, almost monochrome universe; the only colors were soft blues and greens, and the limit of vision was less than thirty meters away. At any one time he could see a dozen slender trunks, supported at regular intervals by the gas-filled bladders that gave them buoyancy, reaching up from the gloomy depths and disappearing into the luminous "sky" overhead. Sometimes he felt that he was walking through a grove of trees on a dull, foggy day; then a school of darting fish destroyed the illusion.

"Two hundred fifty meters," he heard someone call. "We should see the bottom soon. Shall we use the lights? The image quality is deteriorating."

Loren had scarcely noticed any change, because the automatic controls had maintained the picture brilliance. But he realized that it must be almost completely dark at this depth; a human eye would have been virtually useless.

"No—we don't want to disturb anything until we have to. As long as the camera's operating, let's stick to available light."

"There's the bottom! Mostly rock—not much sand."

"Naturally. *Macrocystis thalassi* needs rocks to cling to—it's not like the free-floating *Sargassum.*"

Loren could see what the speaker meant. The slender trunks ended in a network of roots, grasping rock-outcroppings so firmly that no storms or surface currents could dislodge them. The analogy with a forest on land was even closer than he had thought.

Very cautiously, the robot surveyor was working its way into the submarine forest, playing out its cable behind it. There seemed no risk of becoming entangled in the serpentine trunks that reared up to the invisible surface, for there was plenty of space between the giant plants. Indeed, they might have been deliberately—

The scientists looking at the monitor screen realized the incredible truth just a few seconds after Loren.

"Kraken!" one of them whispered. "This isn't a natural forest—it's a—*plantation!*"

29. SABRA

They called themselves Sabras, after the pioneers who, a millennium and a half before, had tamed an almost equally hostile wilderness on Earth.

The Martian Sabras had been lucky in one respect; they had no human enemies to oppose them—only the fierce climate, the barely perceptible atmosphere, the planet-wide sandstorms. All these handicaps they had conquered; they were fond of saying that they had not merely survived, they had prevailed. That quotation was only one of countless borrowings from Earth, which their fierce independence would seldom allow them to acknowledge.

For more than a thousand years, they had lived in the shadow of an illusion—almost a religion. And, like any religion, it had performed an essential role in their society; it had given them goals beyond themselves, and a purpose to their lives.

Until the calculations proved otherwise, they had believed—or at least hoped—that Mars might escape the doom of Earth. It would be a close thing, of course; the extra distance would merely reduce the radiation by fifty percent—but that might be sufficient. Protected by the kilometers of ancient ice at the Poles, perhaps Martians could survive when Men could not. There had even been a fantasy—though only a few romantics had really believed it—that the melting of the polar caps would restore the planet's lost oceans. And then, perhaps, the atmosphere might become dense enough for men to move freely in the open with simple breathing equipment and thermal insulation . . .

These hopes died hard, killed at last by implacable equations. No amount of skill or effort would allow the Sabras to save themselves. They, too, would perish with the mother world whose softness they often affected to despise.

Yet now, spread beneath *Magellan,* was a planet that epitomized all the hopes and dreams of the last generations of Martian colonists. As Owen Fletcher looked down at the endless oceans of Thalassa, one thought kept hammering in his brain.

According to the star-probes, Sagan Two was much like Mars—which was the very reason he and his compatriots had been selected for this voyage. But why resume a battle, three hundred years hence and seventy-five light-years away, when Victory was already here and now?

Fletcher was no longer thinking merely of desertion; that would mean leaving far too much behind. It would be easy enough to hide on Thalassa; but how would he feel, when *Magellan* left, with the last friends and colleagues of his youth?

Twelve Sabras were still in hibernation. Of the five awake, he had already cautiously sounded out two and had received a favorable response. And if the other two also agreed with him, he knew that they could speak for the sleeping dozen.

Magellan must end its starfaring, here at Thalassa.

30. CHILD OF KRAKAN

There was little conversation aboard as *Calypso* headed back toward Tarna at a modest twenty klicks; her passengers were lost in their thoughts, brooding over the implications of those images from the seabed. And Loren was still cut off from the outside world; he had kept on the full-view goggles and was playing back yet again the underwater sledge's exploration of the submarine forest.

Spinning out its cable like a mechanical spider, the robot had moved slowly through the great trunks, which looked slender because of their enormous length but were actually thicker than a man's body. It was now obvious that they were ranged in regular columns and rows, so no one was really surprised when they came to a clearly defined end. And there, going about their business in their jungle encampment, were the scorps.

It had been wise not to switch on the floodlights; the creatures were completely unaware of the silent observer floating in the near darkness only meters overhead. Loren had seen videos of ants, bees, and termites, and the way in which the scorps were functioning reminded him of these. At first sight, it was impossible to believe that such intricate organization could exist without a controlling intelligence—yet their behavior might be entirely automatic, as in the case of Earth's social insects.

Some scorps were tending the great trunks that soared up toward the surface to harvest the rays of the invisible sun; others were scuttling along the seabed carrying rocks, leaves—and yes, crude but unmistakable nets and baskets.

140

So the scorps were tool-makers; but even that did not prove intelligence. Some bird's nests were much more carefully fashioned than these rather clumsy artifacts, apparently constructed from stems and fronds of the omnipresent kelp.

I feel like a visitor from space, Loren thought, poised above a Stone Age village on Earth, just when Man was discovering agriculture. Could he—or it—have correctly assessed human intelligence from such a survey? Or would the verdict have been: pure instinctive behavior?

The probe had now gone so far into the clearing that the surrounding forest was no longer visible, though the nearest trunks could not have been more than fifty meters away. It was then that some wit among the Northers uttered the name that was thereafter unavoidable, even in the scientific reports: "Downtown Scorpville."

It seemed to be, for want of better terms, both a residential and a business area. An outcropping of rock, about five meters high, meandered across the opening, and its face was pierced by numerous dark holes just wide enough to admit a scorp. Although these little caves were irregularly spaced, they were of such uniform size that they could hardly be natural, and the whole effect was that of an apartment building designed by an eccentric architect.

Scorps were coming and going through the entrances—like office workers in one of the old cities before the age of telecommunications, Loren thought. Their activities seemed as meaningless to him as, probably, the commerce of humans would have been to them.

"Hello," one of *Calypso*'s other watchers called, "what's *that*? Extreme right—can you move closer?"

The interruption from outside his sphere of consciousness was jolting; it dragged Loren momentarily from the seabed back to the world of the surface.

His panoramic view tilted abruptly with the probe's change of attitude. Now it was level again and drifting slowly toward an isolated pyramid of rock, which was about ten meters

141

high—judging by the two scorps at its base—and pierced by a single cave entrance. Loren could see nothing unusual about it; then, slowly, he became aware of certain anomalies—jarring elements that did not quite fit into the now-familiar Scorpville scene.

All the other scorps had been busily scurrying about. These two were motionless except for the continual swinging of their heads, back and forth. And there was something else—

These scorps were big. It was hard to judge scale here, and not until several more of the animals had scurried past was Loren quite sure that this pair was almost fifty percent larger than average.

"What are they doing?" somebody whispered.

"I'll tell you," another voice answered. "They're guards—sentries."

Once stated, the conclusion was so obvious that no one doubted it.

"But what are they guarding?"

"The queen, if they have one? The First Bank of Scorpville?"

"How can we find out? The sled's much too big to go inside—even if they'd let us try."

It was at this point that the discussion became academic. The robot probe had now drifted down to within less than ten meters of the pyramid's summit, and the operator gave a brief burst from one of the control jets to stop its descending further.

The sound, or the vibration, must have alerted the sentries. Both of them reared up simultaneously, and Loren had a sudden nightmare vision of clustered eyes, waving palps, and giant claws. I'm glad I'm not *really* here, even though it seems like it, he told himself. And it's lucky they can't swim.

But if they could not swim, they could climb. With astonishing speed, the scorps scrambled up the side of the pyramid and within seconds were on its summit, only a few meters below the sled.

"Gotta get out of here before they jump," the operator said. "Those pinchers could snap our cable like a piece of cotton."

He was too late. A scorp launched itself off the rock, and seconds later its claw grabbed one of the skis of the sled's undercarriage.

The operator's human reflexes were equally swift and in control of a superior technology. At the same instant, he went into full reverse and swung the robot arm downward to the attack. And what was perhaps more decisive, he switched on the floodlights.

The scorp must have been completely blinded. Its claws opened in an almost human gesture of astonishment, and it dropped back to the seabed before the robot's mechanical hand could engage it in combat.

For a fraction of a second, Loren was also blind, as his goggles blacked out. Then the camera's automatic circuits corrected for the increased light level, and he had one startlingly clear close-up of the baffled scorp just before it dropped out of the field of view.

Somehow he was not in the least surprised to see that it was wearing two bands of metal below its right claw.

He was reviewing this final scene as *Calypso* headed back for Tarna, and his senses were still so concentrated on the underwater world that he never felt the mild shockwave as it raced past the boat. But then he became aware of the shouts and confusion around him and felt the deck heel as *Calypso* suddenly changed course. He tore off the goggles and stood blinking in the brilliant sunlight.

For a moment he was totally blind; then, as his eyes adjusted to the glare, he saw that they were only a few hundred meters from South Island's palm-fringed coast. We've hit a reef, he thought. Brant will never hear the last of this . . .

And then he saw, climbing up over the eastern horizon, something he had never dreamed of witnessing on peaceful

143

Thalassa. It was the mushroom cloud that had haunted men's nightmares for two thousand years.

What was Brant *doing*? Surely he should be heading for land; instead, he was swinging *Calypso* around in the tightest possible turning circle, heading out to sea. But he seemed to have taken charge, while everyone else on deck was staring slack-mouthed toward the east.

"Krakan!" one of the Norther scientists whispered, and for a moment Loren thought he was merely using the overworked Lassan expletive. Then he understood, and a vast feeling of relief swept over him. It was very short-lived.

"No," Kumar said, looking more alarmed than Loren would have thought possible. "Not Krakan—much closer. *Child* of Krakan."

The boat radio was now emitting continuous beeps of alarm, interspersed with solemn warning messages. Loren had no time to absorb any of them when he saw that something very strange was happening to the horizon. *It was not where it should have been.*

This was all very confusing; half of his mind was still down there with the scorps, and even now he had to keep blinking against the glare from sea and sky. Perhaps there was something wrong with his vision. Although he was quite certain that *Calypso* was now on an even keel, his eyes told him that it was plunging steeply downward.

No; it was the sea that was rising, with a roar that now obliterated all other sounds. He dared not judge the height of the wave that was bearing down upon them; now he understood why Brant was heading out into deep water, away from the deadly shallows against which the tsunami was about to expend its fury.

A giant hand gripped *Calypso* and lifted her bow up, up toward the zenith. Loren started to slide helplessly along the deck; he tried to grasp a stanchion, missed it, then found himself in the water.

Remember your emergency training, he told himself

144

fiercely. In sea or in space, the principle is always the same. The greatest danger is panic, so keep your head . . .

There was no risk of drowning; his life-jacket would see to that. But where was the inflation lever? His fingers scrabbled wildly around the webbing at his waist, and despite all his resolve, he felt a brief, icy chill before he found the metal bar. It moved easily, and to his great relief he felt the jacket expand around him, gripping him in a welcome embrace.

Now the only real danger would be from *Calypso* herself if she crashed back upon his head. Where was she?

Much too close for comfort, in this raging water, and with part of her deck-housing hanging into the sea. Incredibly, most of the crew still seemed on board. Now they were point-ing at him, and someone was preparing to throw a life-belt.

The water was full of floating debris—chairs, boxes, pieces of equipment—and there went the sled, slowly sinking as it blew bubbles from a damaged buoyancy tank. I hope they can salvage it, Loren thought. If not, this will be a very expensive trip, and it may be a long time before we can study the scorps again. He felt rather proud of himself for so calm an appraisal of the situation, considering the circumstances.

Something brushed against his right leg; with an automatic reflex, he tried to kick it away. Though it bit uncomfortably into the flesh, he was more annoyed than alarmed. He was safely afloat, the giant wave had passed, and nothing could harm him now.

He kicked again, more cautiously. Even as he did so, he felt the same entanglement on the other leg. And now this was no longer a neutral caress; despite the buoyancy of his life-jacket, something was pulling him underwater.

That was when Loren Lorenson felt the first moment of real panic, for he suddenly remembered the questing tentacles of the great polyp. Yet those must be soft and fleshy—this was obviously some wire or cable. Of course—it was the umbilical cord from the sinking sled.

He might still have been able to disentangle himself had he

145

now swallowed a mouthful of water from an unexpected wave. Choking and coughing, he tried to clear his lungs, kicking at the cable at the same time.

And then the vital boundary between air and water—between life and death—was less than a meter overhead; but there was no way that he could reach it.

At such a moment, a man thinks of nothing but his own survival. There were no flashbacks, no regrets for his past life—not even a fleeting glimpse of Mirissa.

When he realized it was all over, he felt no fear. His last conscious thought was pure anger that he had traveled fifty light-years, only to meet so trivial and unheroic an end.

So Loren Lorenson died for the second time in the warm shallows of the Thalassan sea. He had not learned from experience; the first death had been much easier two hundred years ago.

V. THE *BOUNTY* SYNDROME

31. PETITION

Though Capt. Sirdar Bey would have denied that he had a milligram of superstition in his body, he always started to worry when things went well. So far, Thalassa had been almost too good to be true; everything had gone according to the most optimistic plan. The shield was being constructed right on schedule, and there had been absolutely no problems worth talking about.

But now, all within the space of twenty-four hours . . .

Of course, it could have been much worse. Lieutenant Commander Lorenson had been very, very lucky—thanks to that kid. (They'd have to do something for him . . .) According to the medics, it had been extremely close. Another few minuutes and brain damage would have been irreversible.

Annoyed at letting his attention stray from the immediate problem, the captain reread the message he now knew by heart:

SHIPNET: NO DATE NO TIME
TO: CAPTAIN
FROM: ANON
Sir: A number of us wish to make the following proposal, which we put forward for your most serious consideration. We suggest that our mission be terminated here at Thalassa. All its objectives will be realized, without the additional risks involved in proceeding to Sagan Two.
We fully recognize that this will involve problems with the existing population, but we believe they can

149

be solved with the technology we possess—specifically, the use of tectonic engineering to increase the available land area. As per Regulations, Section 14, Para 24 (a), we respectfully request that a Ship's Council be held to discuss this matter as soon as possible.

"Well, Captain Malina? Ambassador Kaldor? Any comments?"

The two guests in the spacious but simply furnished captain's quarters looked at each other simultaneously. Then Kaldor gave an almost imperceptible nod to the deputy captain, and confirmed his relinquishment of priority by taking another slow, deliberate sip of the excellent Thalassan wine their hosts had provided.

Deputy Captain Malina, who was rather more at ease with machines than with people, looked at the printout unhappily.

"At least it's very polite."

"So I should hope," Captain Bey said impatiently. "Have you any idea who could have sent it?"

"None whatsoever. Excluding the three of us, I'm afraid we have 158 suspects."

"157," Kaldor interjected. "Lieutenant Commander Lorenson has an excellent alibi. He was dead at the time."

"That doesn't narrow the field much," the captain said, managing a bleak smile. "Have *you* any theories, Doctor?"

Indeed I have, Kaldor thought. I lived on Mars for two of its long years; my money would be on the Sabras. But that's only a hunch, and I may be wrong . . .

"Not yet, Captain. But I'll keep my eyes open. If I find anything, I'll inform you—as far as possible."

The two officers understood him perfectly. In his role as counsellor, Moses Kaldor was not even responsible to the captain. He was the nearest thing aboard *Magellan* to a father confessor.

"I assume, Dr. Kaldor, that you'll certainly let me know—if you uncover information that could endanger this mission."

Kaldor hesitated, then nodded briefly. He hoped he would not find himself in the traditional dilemma of the priest who received the confession of a murderer—who was still planning his crime.

I'm not getting much help, the captain thought sourly. But I have absolute trust in these two men and need someone to confide in. Even though the final decision must be mine . . .

"The first question is: should I answer this message or ignore it? Either move could be risky. If it's only a casual suggestion—perhaps from a single individual in a moment of psychological disturbance—I might be unwise to take it too seriously. But if it's from a determined group, then perhaps a dialogue may help. It could defuse the situation. It could also identify those concerned." And what would you do then? the Captain asked himself. Clap them in irons?

"I think you should talk to them," Kaldor said. "Problems seldom go away if they're ignored."

"I agree," said Deputy Captain Malina. "But I'm sure it's not any of the Drive or Power crews. I've known all of them since they graduated—or before."

You could be surprised, Kaldor thought. Who ever *really* knows anyone?

"Very well," the captain said, rising to his feet. "That's what I'd already decided. And, just in case, I think I'd better reread some history. I recall that Magellan had a little trouble with his crew."

"Indeed he did," Kaldor answered. "But I trust *you* won't have to maroon anyone."

Or hang one of your commanders, he added to himself; it would have been very tactless to mention that particular piece of history.

And it would be even worse to remind Captain Bey—though surely he could not have forgotten!—that the great navigator had been killed before he could complete his mission.

32. CLINIC

This time, the way back to life had not been prepared so carefully in advance. Loren Lorenson's second awakening was not as comfortable as his first; indeed, it was so unpleasant that he sometimes wished he had been left to sink into oblivion.

When he regained semiconsciousness, he quickly regretted it. There were tubes down his throat and wires attached to his arms and legs. *Wires!* He felt a sudden panic at the memory of that deadly, downward tugging, then brought his emotions under control.

Now there was something else to worry about. He did not seem to be breathing; he could detect no movement of his diaphragm. How very odd—oh, I suppose they've by-passed my lungs—

A nurse must have been alerted by his monitors, for suddenly there was a soft voice in his ear, and he sensed a shadow falling across eyelids that he was still too tired to open.

"You're doing very well, Mister Lorenson. There's nothing to worry about. You'll be up in a few days—No, don't try to talk."

I'd no intention of it, Loren thought. I know exactly what's happened—

Then there was the faint hiss of a hypodermic jet, a brief freezing coldness on his arm, and once more, blessed oblivion.

The next time, to his great relief, everything was quite different. The tubes and wires were gone. Though he felt very weak, he was in no discomfort. And he was breathing again in a steady, normal rhythm.

"Hello," said a deep male voice from a few meters away. "Welcome back."

Loren rolled his head toward the sound and had a blurred glimpse of a bandaged figure in an adjacent bed.

"I guess you don't recognize me, Mister Lorenson. Lieutenant Bill Horton, communications engineer—and exsurfboard rider."

"Oh, hello, Bill—what have *you* been doing—" Loren whispered. But then the nurse arrived and ended that conversation with another well-placed hypodermic.

Now he was perfectly fit and only wanted to be allowed to get up. Surgeon Commander Newton believed that, on the whole, it was best to let her patients know what was happening to them and why. Even if they didn't understand, it helped to keep them quiet so that their annoying presence did not interfere too much with the smooth running of the medical establishment.

"You may *feel* all right, Loren," she said, "but your lungs are still repairing themselves, and you must avoid exertion until they're back to full capacity. If Thalassa's ocean was like Earth's, there would have been no problem. But it's much less saline—it's drinkable, remember, and you drank about a liter of it. And as your body fluids are saltier than the sea, the isotonic balance was all wrong. So there was a good deal of membrane damage through osmotic pressure. We had to do a lot of high-speed research in Ship's Archives before we could handle you. After all, drowning is not a normal space hazard."

"I'll be a good patient," Loren said. "And I certainly appreciate all you've done. But when can I have visitors?"

"There's one waiting outside right now. You can have fifteen minutes. Then nurse will throw her out."

"And don't mind me," Bill Horton said. "I'm fast asleep."

153

33. TIDES

Mirissa felt distinctly unwell, and of course it was all the fault of the Pill. But at least she had the consolation of knowing that this could only happen one more time—when (and if!) she had the second child permitted to her.

It was incredible to think that virtually all the generations of women who had ever existed had been forced to endure these monthly inconveniences for half their lives. Was it pure coincidence, she wondered, that the cycle of fertility approximated that of the Earth's single giant Moon? Just suppose it had worked the same way on Thalassa, with its two close satellites! Perhaps it was just as well that their tides were barely perceptible; the thought of five- and seven-day cycles clashing discordantly together was so comically horrible that she could not help smiling and immediately felt much better.

It had taken her weeks to make the decision, and she had not yet told Loren—still less Brant, busily repairing *Calypso* back on North Island. Would she have done this if he had not left her—for all his bluster and bravado, running away without a fight?

No—that was unfair, a primitive, even prehuman reaction. Yet such instincts died hard; Loren had told her, apologetically, that sometimes he and Brant stalked each other down the corridors of his dreams.

She could not blame Brant; on the contrary, she should be proud of him. It was not cowardice but consideration that had sent him north until they could work out both their destinies.

Her decision had not been made in haste; she realized now that it must have been hovering below the verge of consciousness for weeks. Loren's temporary death had reminded her—as if she needed reminding!—that soon they must part forever. She knew what must be done before he set forth for the stars. Every instinct told her that it was right.

And what would Brant say? How would he react? That was another of the many problems yet to be faced.

I love you, Brant, she whispered. I want you to come back; my second child will be yours.

But not my first.

34. SHIPNET

How odd, thought Owen Fletcher, that I share my name with one of the most famous mutineers of all time! Could I be a descendant? Let's see—it's more than two thousand years since they landed on Pitcairn Island . . . say, a hundred generations, to make it easy . . .

Fletcher took a naive pride in his ability to make mental calculations that, though elementary, surprised and impressed the vast majority; for centuries Man had pushed buttons when faced with the problem of adding two and two. Remembering a few logarithms and mathematical constants helped enormously and made his performance even more mysterious to those who did not know how it was done. Of course, he only chose examples that he knew how to handle, and it was very seldom that anyone bothered to check his answers . . .

A hundred generations back—so two to the hundred ancestors then. Log two is point three zero one zero—that's thirty point one . . . Olympus!—a million, million, million, million, *million* people! Something wrong—nothing like that number ever lived on Earth since the beginning of time—of course, that assumes there was never any overlapping—the human family tree must be hopelessly intertwined—anyway, after a hundred generations everyone must be related to everyone else—I'll never be able to prove it, but Fletcher Christian must be my ancestor—many times over.

All very interesting, he thought, as he switched off the display and the ancient records vanished from the screen. But I'm not a mutineer. I'm a—a—*petitioner*, with a perfectly reasonable request. Karl, Ranjit, Bob, all agree . . . Werner is uncertain but won't give us away. How I wish we could talk to the rest of the Sabras and let them know about the lovely world we've found while they're asleep.

Meanwhile, I have to answer the captain. . . .

Captain Bey found it distinctly unsettling, having to go about the ship's business not knowing who—or how many—of his officers or crew were addressing him through the anonymity of SHIPNET. There was no way that these unlogged inputs could be traced—confidentiality was their very purpose, built in as a stabilizing social mechanism by the long-dead geniuses who had designed *Magellan*. He had tentatively raised the subject of a tracer with his chief communications engineer, but Commander Rocklynn had been so shocked that he had promptly dropped the matter.

So now he was continually searching faces, noting expressions, listening to voice inflections—and trying to behave as if nothing had happened. Perhaps he was overreacting and nothing important *had* happened. But he feared that a seed had been planted, and it would grow and grow with every day the ship remained in orbit above Thalassa.

His first acknowledgment, drafted after consultation with Malina and Kaldor, had been bland enough:

From: CAPTAIN
To: ANON
In reply to your undated communication, I have no objection to discussions along the lines you propose, either through SHIPNET or formally in Ship's Council.

In fact, he had very strong objections; he had spent almost half his adult life training for the awesome responsibility of transplanting a million human beings across a hundred and twenty-five light-years of space. That was his mission; if the

157

word "sacred" had meant anything to him, he would have used it. Nothing short of catastrophic damage to the ship or the unlikely discovery that Sagan Two's sun was about to go nova could possibly deflect him from that goal.

Meanwhile, there was one obvious line of action. Perhaps— like Bligh's men!—the crew was becoming demoralized, or at least slack. The repairs to the ice plant after the minor damage caused by the tsunami had taken twice as long as expected, and that was typical. The whole tempo of the ship was slowing down; yes, it was time to start cracking the whip again.

"Joan," he said to his secretary, thirty thousand kilometers below. "Let me have the latest shield assembly report. And tell Captain Malina I want to discuss the hoisting schedule with him."

He did not know if they could lift more than one snowflake a day. But they could try.

35. CONVALESCENCE

Lieutenant Horton was an amusing companion, but Loren was glad to get rid of him as soon as the electrofusion currents had welded his broken bones. As Loren discovered in somewhat wearisome detail, the young engineer had fallen in with a gang of hairy hunks on North Island, whose second main interest in life appeared to be riding microjet surfboards up vertical waves. Horton had found, the hard way, that it was even more dangerous than it looked.

"I'm quite surprised," Loren had interjected at one point in a rather seamy narrative. "I'd have sworn you were ninety percent hetero."

"Ninety-two, according to my profile," Horton said cheerfully. "But I like to check my calibration from time to time."

The lieutenant was only half joking. Somewhere he had heard that hundred percenters were so rare that they were classed as pathological. Not that he *really* believed it; but it worried him slightly on those very few occasions when he gave the matter any thought.

Now Loren was the sole patient and had convinced the Lassan nurse that her continuous presence was quite unnecessary—at least when Mirissa was paying her daily visit. Surgeon Commander Newton, who like most physicians could be embarrassingly frank, had told him bluntly, "You still need another week to recuperate. If you *must* make love, let her do all the work."

He had many other visitors, of course. With two exceptions, most were welcome.

Mayor Waldron could bully his little nurse to let her in at any time; fortunately, her visitations never coincided with Mirissa's. The first time the mayor arrived, Loren contrived to be in an almost moribund state, but this tactic proved disastrous, as it made it impossible for him to fend off some moist caresses. On the second visit—luckily there had been a ten-minute warning—he was propped up by pillows and fully conscious. However, by a strange coincidence, an elaborate respiratory function test was in progress, and the breathing-tube inserted in Loren's mouth made conversation impossible. The test was completed about thirty seconds after the mayor's departure.

Brant Falconer's one courtesy visit was something of a strain for them both. They talked politely about the scorps, progress at the Mangrove Bay freezing plant, North Island politics—anything, in fact, except Mirissa. Loren could see that Brant was worried, even embarrassed, but the very last thing he expected was an apology. His visitor managed to get it off his chest just before he left.

"You know, Loren," he said reluctantly, "there was nothing else I could have done about that wave. If I'd kept on course, we'd have smashed into the reef. It was just too bad *Calypso* couldn't reach deep water in time."

"I'm quite sure," Loren said with complete sincerity, "that no one could have done a better job."

"Er—I'm glad you understand that."

Brant was obviously relieved, and Loren felt a surge of sympathy—even of pity—for him. Perhaps there had been some criticism of his seamanship; to anyone as proud of his skills as Brant, that would have been intolerable.

"I understand that they've salvaged the sledge."

"Yes—it will soon be repaired, and as good as new."

"Like me."

In the brief comradeship of their joint laughter, Loren was struck by a sudden, ironic thought.

Had Brant, he wondered, ever wished that Kumar had been a little less courageous.

160

36. KILIMANJARO

Why had he dreamed of Kilimanjaro?

It was a strange word; a name, he felt sure—but of what?

Moses Kaldor lay in the gray light of the Thalassan dawn, slowly wakening to the sounds of Tarna. Not that there were many at this hour; a sand-sledge was whirring somewhere on its way to the beach, probably to meet a returning fisherman.

Kilimanjaro.

Kaldor was not a boastful man, but he doubted if any other human being had read quite so many ancient books on such a wide range of subjects. He had also received several terabytes of memory implant, and though information stored that way was not really *knowledge*, it was available if you could recall the access codes.

It was a little early to make the effort, and he doubted if the matter was particularly important. Yet he had learned not to neglect dreams; old Sigmund Freud had made some valid points two thousand years ago. And anyway, he would not be able to get to sleep again. . . .

He closed his eyes, triggered the SEARCH command, and waited. Though that was pure imagination—the process took place at a wholly subconscious level—he could picture myriads of Ks flickering past somewhere in the depths of his brain.

Now something was happening to the phosphenes that forever dance in random patterns on the retina of the tightly closed eye. A dark window had appeared magically in the faintly luminescent chaos; letters were forming—and there it was:

161

ARTHUR C. CLARKE

KILIMANJARO: Volcanic mountain, Africa. Ht. 5.9 km.
Site of first Space Elevator Earth
Terminus.

Well! What did *that* mean? He let his mind play with this
scanty information.

Something to do with that other volcano, Krakan—which
had certainly been in his thoughts a good deal recently? That
seemed rather farfetched. And he needed no warning that
Krakan—or its boisterous offspring—might erupt again.

The first space elevator? That was indeed ancient history;
it marked the very beginning of planetary colonization by giving mankind virtually free access to the Solar System. And
they were employing the same technology here, using cables
of superstrength material to lift the great blocks of ice up to
Magellan as the ship hovered in stationary orbit above the
Equator.

Yet this, too, was a very far cry from that African mountain.
The connection was too remote; the answer, Kaldor felt certain, must be somewhere else

The direct approach had failed. The only way to find the
link—if he ever could—was to leave it to chance and time and
the mysterious workings of the unconscious mind.

He would do his best to forget about Kilimanjaro until it
chose the auspicious time to erupt in his brain.

37. IN VINO VERITAS

Next to Mirissa, Kumar was Loren's most welcome—and most frequent—visitor. Despite his nickname, it seemed to Loren that Kumar was more like a faithful dog—or, rather, a friendly puppy—than a lion. There were a dozen much-pampered dogs in Tarna, and someday they might also live again on Sagan Two, resuming their long acquaintanceship with man.

Loren had now learned what a risk the boy had taken in that tumultuous sea. It was well for them both that Kumar never left shore without a diver's knife strapped to his leg; even so, he had been underwater for more than three minutes, sawing through the cable entangling Loren. *Calypso*'s crew had been certain that they had both drowned.

Despite the bond that now united them, Loren found it difficult to make much conversation with Kumar. After all, there were only a limited number of ways in which one could say, "Thank you for saving my life," and their backgrounds were so utterly dissimilar that they had very few common grounds of reference. If he talked to Kumar about Earth or the ship, everything had to be explained in agonizing detail; and after a while Loren realized that he was wasting his time. Unlike his sister, Kumar lived in the world of immediate experience; only the here and now of Thalassa were important to him. "How I envy him!" Kaldor had once remarked. "He's a creature of today—not haunted by the past or fearful of the future!"

Loren was about to go to sleep on what he hoped would be his last night in the clinic when Kumar arrived carrying a very large bottle, which he held up in triumph.

163

"Guess!"

"I've no idea," Loren said quite untruthfully.

"The first wine of the season, from Krakan. They say it will be a very good year."

"How do *you* know anything about it?"

"Our family's had a vineyard there for more than a hundred years. The Lion Brands are the most famous in the world."

Kumar hunted around until he had produced two glasses and poured generous helpings into each. Loren took a cautious sip; it was a little sweet for his taste but very, *very* smooth.

"What do you call it?" he asked.

"Krakan Special."

"Since Krakan's nearly killed me once, should I risk it?"

"It won't even give you a hangover."

Loren took another, longer draught, and in a surprisingly short time the glass was empty. In an even shorter time it was full again.

This seemed an excellent way of spending his last night in hospital, and Loren felt his normal gratitude toward Kumar extending to the entire world. Even one of Mayor Waldron's visits would no longer be unwelcome.

"By the way, how is Brant? I haven't seen him for a week."

"Still on North Island, arranging repairs to the boat and talking to the marine biologists. Everyone's very excited about the scorps. But no one can decide what to do about them. If anything."

"You know, I feel rather the same way about Brant."

Kumar laughed.

"Don't worry. He's got a girl on North Island."

"Oh. Does Mirissa know?"

"Of course."

"And she doesn't mind?"

"Why should she? Brant loves her—and he always comes back."

Loren processed this information, though rather slowly. It

occurred to him that he was a new variable in an already complex equation. Did Mirissa have any other lovers? Did he really want to know? Should he ask?

"Anyway," Kumar continued as he refilled both their glasses, "all that really matters is that their gene maps have been approved, and they've been registered for a son. When he's born, it will be different. Then they'll only need each other. Wasn't it the same on Earth?"

"Sometimes," Loren said. So Kumar doesn't know; the secret was still between the two of them.

At least I will see my son, Loren thought, if only for a few months. And then . . .

To his horror, he felt tears trickling down his cheeks. When had he last cried? Two hundred years ago, looking back on the burning Earth . . .

"What's the matter?" Kumar asked. "Are you thinking about your wife?" His concern was so genuine that Loren found it impossible to take offense at his bluntness—or at his reference to a subject that, by mutual consent, was seldom mentioned, because it had nothing to do with the here and now. Two hundred years ago on Earth and three hundred years hence on Sagan Two were too far from Thalassa for his emotions to grasp, especially in his present somewhat bemused condition.

"No, Kumar, I was *not* thinking of—my wife—"

"Will you . . . ever . . . tell her . . . about Mirissa?"

"Perhaps. Perhaps not. I really don't know. I feel very sleepy. Did we drink the whole bottle? Kumar? Kumar!"

The nurse came in during the night, and suppressing her giggles, tucked in the sheets so that they would not fall out.

Loren woke first. After the initial shock of recognition, he started to laugh.

"What's so funny?" Kumar said, heaving himself rather blearily out of bed.

165

"If you really want to know—I was wondering if Mirissa would be jealous."

Kumar grinned wryly.

"I may have been a little drunk," he said, "but I'm quite sure that nothing happened."

"So am I."

Yet he realized that he loved Kumar—not because he had saved his life or even because he was Mirissa's brother—but simply because he was Kumar. Sex had absolutely nothing to do with it; the very idea would have filled them not with embarrassment but hilarity. That was just as well. Life on Tarna was already sufficiently complicated.

"And you were right," Loren added, "about the Krakan Special. I don't have a hangover. In fact, I feel wonderful. Can you send a few bottles up to the ship? Better still—a few hundred liters."

38. DEBATE

It was a simple question, but it did not have a simple answer: What would happen to discipline aboard *Magellan* if the very purpose of the ship's mission was put to the vote?

Of course, any result would not be binding, and he could override it if necessary. He would *have* to if a majority decided to stay (not that for a moment he imagined . . .) But such an outcome would be psychologically devastating. The crew would be divided into two factions, and that could lead to situations he preferred not to contemplate.

And yet—a commander had to be firm but not pigheaded. There was a good deal of sense in the proposal, and it had many attractions. After all, he had enjoyed the benefits of presidential hospitality himself and had every intention of meeting that lady decathlon champion again. This was a beautiful world; perhaps they could speed up the slow process of continent building so that there was room for the extra millions. It would be infinitely easier than colonizing Sagan Two.

For that matter, they might never reach Sagan Two. Although the ship's operational reliability was still estimated to be ninety-eight percent, there were external hazards that no one could predict. Only a few of his most trusted officers knew about the section of the ice-shield that had been lost somewhere around light-year forty-eight. If that interstellar meteoroid, or whatever it was, had been just a few meters closer . . .

Someone had suggested that the thing could have been an ancient space-probe from Earth. The odds against this were literally astronomical, and of course such an ironic hypothesis could never be proved.

And now his unknown petitioners were calling themselves the New Thalassans. Did that mean, Captain Bey wondered, that there were many of them and they were getting organized into a political movement? If so, perhaps the best thing would be to get them out into the open as soon as possible.

Yes, it was time to call Ship's Council.

Moses Kaldor's rejection had been swift and courteous.

"No, Captain; I can't get involved in the debate—pro or con. If I did, the crew would no longer trust my impartiality. But I'm willing to act as chairman, or moderator—whatever you like to call it."

"Agreed," Captain Bey said promptly; this was as much as he had really hoped for. "And who will present the motions? We can't expect the New Thalassans to come out into the open and plead their case."

"I wish we could have a straight vote without any arguments and discussions," Deputy Captain Malina had lamented.

Privately, Captain Bey agreed. But this was a democratic society of responsible, highly educated men, and Ship's Orders recognized that fact. The New Thalassans had asked for a Council to air their views; if he refused, he would be disobeying his own letters of appointment and violating the trust given him on Earth two hundred years ago.

It had not been easy to arrange the Council. Since everyone, without exception, had to be given a chance of voting, schedules and duty rosters had to be reorganized and sleep periods disrupted. The fact that half the crew was down on Thalassa presented another problem that had never arisen before—that of security. Whatever its outcome might be, it was highly undesirable that the Lassans overhear the debate . . .

And so Loren Lorenson was alone, with the door of his Tarna office locked for the first time he could recall, when the

Council began. Once again he was wearing full-view goggles; but this time he was not drifting through a submarine forest. He was aboard *Magellan*, in the familiar Assembly room, looking at the faces of colleagues, and whenever he switched his viewpoint, at the screen on which their comments and their verdict would be displayed. At the moment it bore one brief message:

> RESOLVED: That the Starship *Magellan* terminate its
> mission at Thalassa as all its prime objectives can
> be achieved here.

So Moses is up on the ship, Loren thought as he scanned the audience; I wondered why I'd not seen him lately. He looks tired—and so does the captain. Maybe this is more serious than I'd imagined. . . .

Kaldor rapped briskly for attention.

"Captain, officers, fellow crewmembers—although this is our first Council, you all know the rules of procedure. If you wish to speak, hold up your hand to be recognized. If you wish to make a written statement, use your keypad; the addresses have been scrambled to ensure anonymity. In either case, please be as brief as possible.

"If there are no questions, we will open with Item zero zero one."

The New Thalassans had added a few arguments, but essentially 001 was still the memorandum that had jolted Captain Bey two weeks ago—a period in which he had made no progress at all in discovering its authorship.

Perhaps the most telling additional point was the suggestion that it was their *duty* to stay here; Lassa *needed* them, technically, culturally, genetically. I wonder, Loren thought, tempted though he was to agree. In any event, we should ask their opinion first. We're not old-style imperialists—or are we?

Everyone had had time to reread the memorandum; Kaldor rapped for attention again.

"No one has, ah, requested permission to speak in favor of the resolution; of course, there will be opportunities later. So I will ask Lieutenant Elgar to put the case against."

Raymond Elgar was a thoughtful young Power and Communications engineer whom Loren knew only slightly; he had musical talents and claimed to be writing an epic poem about the voyage. When challenged to produce even a single verse, he invariably replied, "Wait until Sagan Two plus one year."

It was obvious why Lieutenant Elgar had volunteered (if indeed he had volunteered) for this role. His poetic pretensions would hardly allow him to do otherwise; and perhaps he really was working on that epic.

"Captain—shipmates—lend me your ears—"

That's a striking phrase, Loren thought. I wonder if it's original?

"I think we will all agree, in our hearts as well as our minds, that the idea of remaining on Thalassa has a great many attractions. But consider these points:

"There are only 161 of us. Have we the right to make an irrevocable decision for the million who are still sleeping?

"And what of the Lassans? It's been suggested that we'll help them by staying on. But will we? They have a way of life that seems to suit them perfectly. Consider *our* background, our training—the goal to which we dedicated ourselves years ago. Do you really imagine that a million of us could become part of Thalassan society without disrupting it completely?

"And there is the question of duty. Generations of men and women sacrificed themselves to make this mission possible— to give the human race a better chance of survival. The more suns we reach, the greater our insurance against disaster. We have seen what the Thalassan volcanoes can do; who knows what may happen here in the centuries to come?

"There has been glib talk of tectonic engineering to make new land, to provide room for the increased population. May I remind you that even on Earth, after thousands of years of research and development, that was still not an exact science.

170

Remember the Nazca Plate Catastrophe of 3175! I can imagine nothing more reckless than to meddle with the forces pent up inside Thalassa.

"There's no need to say any more. There can be only one decision in this matter. We must leave the Lassans to their own destiny; *we* have to go on to Sagan Two."

Loren was not surprised at the slowly mounting applause. The interesting question was: Who had *not* joined it? As far as he could judge, the audience was almost equally divided. Of course, some people might be applauding because they admired the very effective presentation—not necessarily because they agreed with the speaker.

"Thank you, Lieutenant Elgar," Chairman Kaldor said. "We particularly appreciate your brevity. Now would anyone like to express the contrary opinion?"

There was an uneasy stirring followed by a profound silence. For at least a minute, nothing happened. Then letters began to appear on the screen.

002. WOULD THE CAPTAIN PLEASE GIVE THE LATEST ESTIMATE OF PROBABLE MISSION SUCCESS

003. WHY NOT REVIVE A REPRESENTATIVE SAMPLE OF THE SLEEPERS TO POLL THEIR OPINION

004. WHY NOT ASK THE LASSANS WHAT THEY THINK. IT'S THEIR WORLD

With total secrecy and neutrality, the computer stored and numbered the inputs from the Council members. In two millennia, no one had been able to invent a better way of sampling group opinion and obtaining a consensus. All over the ship—and down on Thalassa—men and women were tapping out messages on the seven buttons of their little one-hand keypads. Perhaps the earliest skill acquired by any child was the

171

ability to touch-type all the necessary combinations without even thinking about them.

Loren swept his eye across the audience and was amused to note that almost everyone had both hands in full view. He could see nobody with the typical far-off look, indicating that a private message was being transmitted via a concealed keypad. But somehow a lot of people were talking.

> 015. WHAT ABOUT A COMPROMISE? SOME OF US MIGHT PREFER TO STAY. THE SHIP COULD GO ON

Kaldor rapped for attention.

"That's not the resolution we're discussing," he said, "but it's been noted."

"To answer Zero Zero Two," Captain Bey said, barely remembering in time to get a go-ahead nod from the chairman, "the figure is ninety-eight percent. I wouldn't be surprised if our chance of reaching Sagan Two is better than that of North or South Island staying above water."

> 021. APART FROM KRAKAN, WHICH THEY CAN'T DO MUCH ABOUT, THE LASSANS DON'T HAVE ANY SERIOUS CHALLENGES. MAYBE WE SHOULD LEAVE THEM SOME. KNR

That would be, let's see . . . Of course—Kingsley Rasmussen. Obviously he had no wish to remain incognito. He was expressing a thought that at one time or other had occurred to almost everyone.

> 022. WE'VE ALREADY SUGGESTED THEY REBUILD THE DEEP SPACE ANTENNA ON KRAKAN TO KEEP IN TOUCH WITH US. RMM

> 023. A TEN YEAR JOB AT THE MOST. KNR

"Gentlemen," Kaldor said a little impatiently, "we're getting away from the point."

Have I anything to contribute? Loren asked himself. No, I will sit out this debate; I can see too many sides. Sooner or later I will have to choose between duty and happiness. But not yet. Not yet . . .

"I'm quite surprised," Kaldor said after nothing more had appeared on the screen for a full two minutes, "that no one has anything more to say on such an important matter."

He waited hopefully for another minute.

"Very well. Perhaps you'd like to continue the discussion informally. We will not take a vote now, but during the next forty-eight hours you can record your opinion in the usual way. Thank you."

He glanced at Captain Bey, who rose to his feet with a swiftness that showed his obvious relief.

"Thank you, Dr. Kaldor. Ship's Council terminated."

Then he looked anxiously at Kaldor, who was staring at the display screen as if he had just noticed it for the first time.

"Are you all right, Doctor?"

"Sorry, Captain—I'm fine. I've just remembered something important, that's all."

Indeed he had. For the thousandth time, at least, he marveled at the labyrinthine workings of the subconscious mind.

Entry 021 had done it. "The Lassans don't have any serious challenges."

Now he knew why he had dreamed of Kilimanjaro.

39. THE LEOPARD IN THE SNOWS

I'm sorry, Evelyn—it's been many days since I last talked to you. Does this mean that your image is fading in my mind as the future absorbs more and more of my energies and attention?

I suppose so, and logically I should welcome it. Clinging too long to the past is a sickness—as you often reminded me. But in my heart I still can't accept that bitter truth.

Much has happened in the last few weeks. The ship has been infected with what I call the *Bounty* Syndrome. We should have anticipated it—indeed, we did, but only as a joke. Now it's serious, though so far not too serious. I hope.

Some of the crew would like to remain on Thalassa—who can blame them?—and have frankly admitted it. Others want to terminate the whole mission here and forget about Sagan Two. We don't know the strength of this faction, because it hasn't come out into the open.

Forty-eight hours after the Council, we had the vote. Although of course the balloting was secret, I don't know how far the results can be trusted. 151 were for going on; only 6 wanted to terminate the mission here; and there were 4 undecideds.

Captain Bey was pleased. He feels the situation's under control but is going to take some precautions. He realizes that the longer we stay here, the greater the pressure will be not to leave at all. He won't mind a few deserters—"If they want to go, I certainly don't want to keep them," was the way he put it. But he's worried about disaffection spreading to the rest of the crew.

So he's accelerating shield construction. Now that the system is completely automatic and running smoothly, we plan to make two lifts a day instead of one. If this works out, we can leave in four months. This hasn't been announced yet. I hope there are no protests when it is, from the New Lassans or anyone else.

And now another matter that may be completely unimportant but which I find fascinating. Do you remember how we used to read stories to each other when we first met? It was a wonderful way of getting to know how people really lived and thought thousands of years ago—long before sensory or even video recordings existed . . .

Once you read to me—I had not the slightest *conscious* memory of it—a story about a great mountain in Africa with a strange name, Kilimanjaro. I've looked it up in Ship's Archives, and now I understand why it's been haunting me.

It seems that there was a cave high up on the mountain, above the snow line. And in that cave was the frozen body of a great hunting cat—a leopard. That's the mystery; no one ever knew what the leopard was doing at such an altitude, so far from its normal territory.

You know, Evelyn, that I was always proud—many people said vain!—about my powers of intuition. Well, it seems to me that something like this is happening here.

Not once but several times, a large and powerful marine animal has been detected a long way from its natural habitat. Recently, the first one was captured; it's a kind of huge crustacean, like the sea scorpions that once lived on Earth.

We're not sure if they're intelligent, and that may even be a meaningless question. But certainly they are highly organized social animals, with primitive technologies—though perhaps that's too strong a word. As far as we've discovered, they don't show any greater abilities than bees or ants or termites, but their scale of operations is different and quite impressive.

Most important of all, they've discovered metal, though as

175

yet they seem to use it only for ornament, and their sole source of supply is what they can steal from the Lassans. They've done this several times.

And recently a scorp crawled up the channel right into the heart of our freezing plant. The naive assumption was that it was hunting for food. But there was plenty where it came from—at least fifty kilometers away.

I want to know what that scorp was doing so far from home; I feel that the answer may be very important to the Lassans.

I wonder if we'll find it before I begin the long sleep to Sagan Two.

40. CONFRONTATION

The instant that Captain Bey walked into President Farradine's office, he knew that something was wrong.

Normally, Edgar Farradine greeted him by his first name and immediately produced the wine decanter. This time there was no "Sirdar," and no wine, but at least he was offered a chair.

"I've just received some disturbing news, Captain Bey. If you don't mind, I'd like the prime minister to join us."

This was the first time the captain had ever heard the president come straight to the point—*whatever* it was—and also the first time he had met the PM in Farradine's office.

"In that case, Mr. President, may I ask Ambassador Kaldor to join me?"

The president hesitated only a moment; then he replied, "Certainly." The captain was relieved to see a ghost of a smile, as if in recognition of this diplomatic nicety. The visitors might be outranked—but not outnumbered.

Prime Minister Bergman, as Captain Bey knew perfectly well, was really the power behind the throne. Behind the PM was the cabinet, and behind the cabinet was the Jefferson Mark 3 Constitution. The arrangement had worked well for the last few centuries; Captain Bey had a foreboding that it was now about to undergo some major perturbation.

Kaldor was quickly rescued from Mrs. Farradine, who was using him as a guinea pig to try out her ideas for redecorating the President's House. The prime minister arrived a few seconds later, wearing his usual inscrutable expression.

When they were all seated, the president folded his arms,

leaned back in his ornate swivel chair, and looked accusingly at his visitors.

"Captain Bey—Dr. Kaldor—we have received some most disturbing information. We would like to know if there is any truth in the report that you now intend to end your mission here—and *not* at Sagan Two."

Captain Bey felt a great sensation of relief—followed instantly by annoyance. There must have been a bad breach of security; he had hoped that the Lassans would never hear of the petition and Ship's Council—though perhaps that was too much to expect.

"Mr. President—Mr. Prime Minister—if you have heard such a rumor, I can assure you that there is absolutely no truth in it. Why do you think we are hoisting six hundred tons of ice a day to rebuild our shield? Would we bother to do that if we planned to stay here?"

"Perhaps. If for some reason you've changed your mind, you would hardly alert us by suspending operations."

The quick rejoiner gave the captain a momentary shock; he had underrated these amiable people. Then he realized that they—and their computers—must have already analyzed all the obvious possibilities.

"True enough. But I'd like to tell you—it's still confidential and not yet announced—that we plan to double the rate of hoisting to finish the shield more quickly. Far from staying on, we plan to leave early. I had hoped to inform you of this in more pleasant circumstances."

Even the prime minister could not completely conceal his surprise; the president did not even try. Before they could recover, Captain Bey resumed his attack:

"And it's only fair, Mr. President, that you give us the evidence for your—accusation. Otherwise, how can we refute it?"

The president looked at the prime minister. The prime minister looked at the visitors.

"I'm afraid that's impossible. It would reveal our sources of information."

"Then it's a stalemate. We won't be able to convince you until we really do leave—one hundred and thirty days from now according to the revised schedule."

There was a thoughtful and rather gloomy silence; then Kaldor said quietly: "Could I have a brief private talk with the captain?"

"Of course."

While they were gone, the president asked the prime minister: "Are they telling the truth?"

"Kaldor wouldn't lie; I'm certain of that. But perhaps he doesn't know all the facts."

There was no time to continue the discussion before the parties of the second part returned to face their accusers.

"Mr. President," the captain said, "Dr. Kaldor and I both agree that there is something we should tell you. We'd hoped to keep it quiet—it was embarrassing and we thought the matter had been settled. Possibly we're wrong; in that case, we may need your help."

He gave a brief summary of the Council proceedings and the events that had led up to them and concluded, "If you wish, I'm prepared to show you the recordings. We have nothing to hide."

"That won't be necessary, Sirdar," the president said, obviously vastly relieved. The prime minister, however, still looked worried.

"Er—just a minute, Mr. President. That doesn't dispose of the reports we've received. They were very convincing, you'll recall."

"I'm sure the captain will be able to explain them."

"Only if you tell me what they are."

There was another pause. Then the president moved toward the wine decanter.

"Let's have a drink first," he said cheerfully. "Then I'll tell you how we found out."

179

41. PILLOW TALK

It had gone very smoothly, Owen Fletcher told himself. Of course, he was somewhat disappointed by the vote, though he wondered how accurately it reflected opinion aboard the ship. After all, he had instructed two of his fellow conspirators to register noes, lest the—still-pitiful—strength of the New Thalassan movement be revealed.

What to do next was, as always, the problem. He was an engineer, not a politician—though he was rapidly moving in that direction—and could see no way of recruiting further support without coming out into the open.

This left only two alternatives. The first, and easier, was to jump ship, as close to launch-time as possible, by simply failing to report back. Captain Bey would be too busy to hunt for them—even if he felt inclined—and their Lassan friends would hide them until *Magellan*'s departure.

But that would be a double desertion—one unheard of in the closely knit Sabra community. He would have abandoned his sleeping colleagues—including his own brother and sister. What would they think of him, three centuries hence on hostile Sagan Two, when they learned that he could have opened the gates of Paradise for them but had failed to do so?

And now the time was running out; those computer simulations of up-rated lifting schedules could have only one meaning. Though he had not even discussed this with his friends, he saw no alternative to action.

But his mind still shied away from the word *sabotage*.

Rose Killian had never heard of Delilah and would have been

horrified to be compared to her. She was a simple, rather naive Norther who—like so many young Lassans—had been overwhelmed by the glamorous visitors from Earth. Her affair with Karl Bosley was not only her first really profound emotional experience; it was also his.

They were both heartsick at the thought of parting. Rose was weeping on Karl's shoulder late one night when he could bear her misery no longer.

"Promise not to tell *anyone*," he said, fondling the strands of hair lying along his chest. "I've some good news for you. It's a big secret—nobody knows it yet. The ship isn't going to leave. We're all staying here on Thalassa."

Rose almost fell off the bed in her surprise.

"You're not saying this just to make me happy?"

"No—it's true. But don't say a word to anyone. It must be kept *completely* secret."

"Of course, darling."

But Rose's closest friend Marion was also weeping for *her* Earth lover, so she had to be told. . . .

. . . and Marion passed the good news on to Pauline . . . who couldn't resist telling Svetlana . . . who mentioned it in confidence to Crystal.

And Crystal was the president's daughter.

181

42. SURVIVOR

This is a very unhappy business, Captain Bey thought. Owen Fletcher is a good man; I approved his selection myself. How could he have done such a thing?

There was probably no single explanation. If he had not been a Sabra *and* in love with that girl, it might never have happened. What was the word for one plus one adding up to more than two? Sin-something—ah, yes, synergy. Yet he could not help feeling that there was something more, something that he would probably never know.

He remembered a remark that Kaldor, who always had a phrase for every occasion, had made to him once when they were talking about crew psychology.

"We're all *maimed*, Captain, whether we admit it or not. No one who's been through our experiences during those last years on Earth could possibly be unaffected. And we all share the same feeling of guilt."

"Guilt?" he had asked in surprise and indignation.

"Yes, even though it's not our fault. We're survivors—the *only* survivors. And survivors always feel guilty at being alive."

It was a disturbing remark, and it might help to explain Fletcher—and many other things.

We're all maimed men.

I wonder what your injury is, Moses Kaldor—and how you handle it. I know mine and have been able to use it for the benefit of my fellow humans. It brought me to where I am today, and I can be proud of that.

Perhaps in an earlier age I might have been a dictator, or a

182

warlord. Instead, I have been usefully employed as Chief of Continental Police, as General-in-Charge of Space Construction Facilities—and finally as commander of a starship. My fantasies of power have been successfully sublimated.

He walked to the captain's safe, to which he alone held the key, and slipped the coded metal bar into its slot. The door swung smoothly open to reveal assorted bundles of papers, some medals and trophies, and a small, flat wooden box bearing the letters S.B. inlaid in silver.

As the captain placed it on the table, he was happy to feel the familiar stirring in his loins. He opened the lid and stared down at the gleaming instrument of power, snug in its velvet bed.

Once his perversion had been shared by millions. Usually it was quite harmless—in primitive societies, even valuable. And many times it had changed the course of history, for better or for worse.

"I know you're a phallic symbol," the captain whispered. "But you're also a gun. I've used you before; I can use you again . . ."

The flashback could not have lasted for more than a fraction of a second, yet it seemed to cover years of time. He was still standing by his desk when it was over; just for a moment, all the careful work of the psychotherapists was undone, and the gates of memory opened wide.

He looked back in horror—yet with fascination—on those last turbulent decades, which had brought out the best and the worst in humanity. He remembered how, as a young Inspector of Police in Cairo, he had given his first order to fire on a rioting crowd. The bullets were supposed to be merely incapacitating. But two people had died.

What had they been rioting about? He had never even known—there were so many political and religious movements in the final days. And it was also the great era of the supercriminals; they had nothing to lose and no future to look forward to, so they were prepared to take any risks. Most of them had been psychopaths, but some had been near geniuses. He thought of Joseph Kidder, who had almost stolen a starship. No one knew what had happened to him, and sometimes Captain Bey had been struck by a nightmare fantasy: "Just suppose that one of my sleepers is *really* . . ."

The forcible running down of the population, the total prohibition of any new births after the year 3600, the absolute priority given to the development of the quantum drive and the building of the *Magellan*-class ships—all these pressures, together with the knowledge of impending doom, had imposed such strains on terrestrial society that it still seemed a miracle that anyone had been able to escape from the Solar System. Captain Bey remembered, with admiration and gratitude, those who had burned up their last years for a cause whose success or failure they would never know.

He could see again the last world president, Elizabeth Windsor, exhausted but proud as she left the ship after her tour of inspection, returning to a planet that had only days to live. She had even less time; the bomb in her spaceplane had exploded just before it was due to land at Port Canaveral.

The captain's blood still ran cold at the memory; that bomb had been intended for *Magellan*, and only a mistake in timing had saved the ship. It was ironic that each of the rival cults had claimed responsibility . . .

Jonathan Cauldwell and his dwindling but still vocal band of followers proclaimed ever more desperately that all would be well, that God was merely testing Mankind as He had once tested Job. Despite everything that was happening to the Sun, it would soon return to normal, and humanity would be saved—unless those who disbelieved in His mercy provoked His wrath. And *then* He might change His mind . . .

The Will of God cult believed the exact opposite. Doomsday had come at last, and no attempt should be made to avoid it. Indeed, it should be welcomed, since after Judgment those who were worthy of salvation would live in eternal bliss.

And so, from totally opposing premises, the Cauldwellites

and the WOGs arrived at the same conclusion: The human race should not attempt to escape its destiny. All starships should be destroyed.

Perhaps it was fortunate that the two rival cults were so bitterly opposed that they could not cooperate even toward a goal that they both shared. In fact, after the death of President Windsor their hostility turned to internecine violence. The rumor was started—almost certainly by the World Security Bureau, though Bey's colleagues had never admitted it to him—that the bomb had been planted by the WOGs and its timer sabotaged by the Cauldwellites. The exactly opposite version was also popular; one of them might even have been true.

All this was history, now known only to a handful of men besides himself and soon to be forgotten. Yet how strange that *Magellan* was once again threatened by sabotage.

Unlike the WOGs and the Cauldwellites, the Sabras were highly competent and not unhinged by fanaticism. They could therefore be a more serious problem, but Captain Bey believed he knew how to handle it.

You're a good man, Owen Fletcher, he thought grimly. But I've killed better ones in my time. And when there was no alternative, I've used torture.

He was more than a little proud of the fact that he had never enjoyed it; and this time, there was a better way.

43. INTERROGATION

And now *Magellan* had a new crewmember, untimely awakened from his slumber and still adjusting to the realities of the situation—as Kaldor had done a year ago. Nothing but an emergency justified such action. But according to the computer records only Dr. Marcus Steiner, once Chief Scientist of the Terran Bureau of Investigation, possessed the knowledge and skills that, unfortunately, were needed now.

Back on Earth, his friends had often asked him why he had chosen to become a professor of criminology. And he had always given the same answer: "The only alternative was to become a criminal."

It had taken Steiner almost a week to modify the sickbay's standard encephalographic equipment and to check the computer programs. Meanwhile, the four Sabras remained confined to their quarters and stubbornly refused to make any admissions of guilt.

Owen Fletcher did not look very happy when he saw the preparations that had been made for him; there were too many similarities to electric chairs and torture devices from the bloodstained history of Earth. Dr. Steiner quickly put him at ease with the synthetic familiarity of the good interrogator.

"There's nothing to be alarmed at, Owen—I promise you won't feel a thing. You won't even be aware of the answers you're giving me—but there's no way you can hide the truth. Because you're an intelligent man, I'll tell you *exactly* what I'm going to do. Surprisingly enough, it helps me do my job; whether *you* like it or not, your subconscious mind will trust me—and cooperate."

What nonsense, thought Lieutenant Fletcher; surely he doesn't think he can fool me as easily as that! But he made no reply, as he was seated in the chair and the orderlies fastened leather straps loosely around his forearms and waist. He did not attempt to resist; two of his largest excolleagues were standing uncomfortably in the background, carefully avoiding his eye.

"If you need a drink or want to go to the toilet, just say so. This first session will take exactly one hour; we may need some shorter ones later. We want to make you relaxed and comfortable."

In the circumstances, this was a highly optimistic remark, but no one seemed to think it at all funny.

"Sorry we've had to shave your head, but scalp electrodes don't like hair. And you'll have to be blindfolded so we don't pick up confusing visual inputs . . . Now you'll start getting drowsy, but you'll remain perfectly conscious . . . We're going to ask you a series of questions which have just three possible answers—Yes, no, or don't know. But you won't have to reply; your brain will do it for you, and the computer's trinary logic system will know what it's saying.

"And there's absolutely no way you can lie to us; you're very welcome to try! Believe me, some of the best minds of Earth invented this machine—and were never able to fool it. If it gets ambiguous answers, the computer will simply reframe the questions. Are you ready? Very well . . . Recorder on high, please . . . Check gain on Channel 5 . . . Run the program."

YOUR NAME IS OWEN FLETCHER . . . ANSWER YES . . . OR NO . . .
YOUR NAME IS JOHN SMITH . . . ANSWER YES . . . OR NO . . .
YOU WERE BORN IN LOWELL CITY, MARS . . . ANSWER YES . . . OR NO . . .

YOUR NAME IS JOHN SMITH . . . ANSWER YES . . .
 OR NO . . .
YOU WERE BORN IN AUCKLAND, NEW ZEALAND . . .
 ANSWER YES . . . OR NO . . .
YOUR NAME IS OWEN FLETCHER . . .
YOU WERE BORN ON 3 MARCH 3585 . . .
YOU WERE BORN ON 31 DECEMBER 3584 . . .

The questions came at such short intervals that even if he had not been in a mildly sedated condition, Fletcher would have been unable to falsify the answers. Nor would it have mattered had he done so; within a few minutes, the computer had established the pattern of his automatic responses to all the questions whose answers were already known.

From time to time the calibration was rechecked (YOUR NAME IS OWEN FLETCHER . . . YOU WERE BORN IN CAPE-TOWN, ZULULAND . . .), and questions were occasionally repeated to confirm answers already given. The whole process was completely automatic, once the physiological constellation of YES–NO responses had been identified.

The primitive 'lie detectors' had tried to do this with fair success—but seldom complete certainty. It had taken no more than two hundred years to perfect the technology and thereby to revolutionize the practice of law, both criminal and civil, to the point when few trials ever lasted more than hours.

It was not so much an interrogation as a computerized— and cheat-proof—version of the ancient game Twenty Questions. In principle, *any* piece of information could be quickly pinned down by a series of YES–NO replies, and it was surprising how seldom as many as twenty were needed when an expert human cooperated with an expert machine.

When a rather dazed Owen Fletcher staggered from the chair, exactly one hour later, he had no idea what he had been asked or how he had responded. He was fairly confident, however, that he had given nothing away.

He was mildly surprised when Dr. Steiner said cheerfully, "That's it, Owen. We won't need you again."

The professor was proud of the fact that he had never hurt anybody, but a good interrogator had to be something of a sadist—if only a psychological one. Besides, it added to his reputation for infallibility, and that was half the battle.

He waited until Fletcher had regained his balance and was being escorted back to the detention cell.

"Oh, by the way, Owen—that trick with the ice would never have worked."

In fact, it might well have; but that didn't matter now. The expression on Lieutenant Fletcher's face gave Dr. Steiner all the reward he needed for the exercise of his considerable skills.

Now he could go back to sleep until Sagan Two. But first he would relax and enjoy himself, making the most of this unexpected interlude.

Tomorrow he would have a look at Thalassa and perhaps go swimming off one of those beautiful beaches. But for the moment he would enjoy the company of an old and beloved friend.

The book he drew reverently out of its vacuum-sealed package was not merely a first edition; it was now the *only* edition. He opened it at random; after all, he knew practically every page by heart.

He started to read, and fifty light-years from the ruins of Earth, the fog rolled once more down Baker Street.

"The cross-checking has confirmed that only the four Sabras were involved," Captain Bey said. "We can be thankful that there's no need to interrogate anyone else."

"I still don't understand how they hoped to get away with it," Deputy Captain Malina said unhappily.

"I don't believe they would, but it's lucky it was never put to the test. Anyway, they were still undecided.

"Plan A involved damaging the shield. As you know, Fletcher was on the assembly crew and was working out a scheme to reprogram the last stage of the lifting procedure. If a block of ice could be allowed to impact at just a few meters a second—you see what I mean?

"It could be made to look like an accident, but there was a risk that the subsequent inquiry would soon prove it was nothing of the sort. And even if the shield was damaged, it could be repaired. Fletcher hoped that the delay would give time to acquire more recruits. He might have been right; another year on Thalassa . . .

"Plan B involved sabotaging the life-support system so that the ship had to be evacuated. Again, the same objections.

"Plan C was the most disturbing one because it would have terminated the mission. Luckily, none of the Sabras was in Propulsion; it would have been very hard for them to get at the drive . . ."

Everyone looked shocked—though none more so than Commander Rocklynn.

"It would not have been at all difficult, sir, if they were sufficiently determined. The big problem would have been to arrange something that would put the drive out of action—*permanently*—without damaging the ship. I very much doubt if they'd have the technical knowledge necessary."

"They were working on it," the captain grimly said. "We have to review our security proceedings, I'm afraid. There will be a conference on that tomorrow for all senior officers—here, at noon."

And then Surgeon Commander Newton put the question that everyone hesitated to ask.

"Will there be a court martial, Captain?"

"It's not necessary; guilt has been established. According to Ship's Orders, the only problem is the sentence."

Everyone waited. And waited.

"Thank you, ladies and gentlemen," the captain said, and his officers left in silence.

Alone in his quarters, he felt angry and betrayed. But at

least it was over; *Magellan* had ridden out the man-made storm.

The other three Sabras were—perhaps—harmless; but what about Owen Fletcher?

His mind strayed to the deadly plaything in his safe. He was captain: it would be easy to arrange an accident . . .

He put the fantasy aside; he could never do it, of course. In any event, he had already made up his mind and was certain that there would be universal agreement.

Someone had once said that for every problem there is a solution that is simple, attractive—and wrong. But this solution, he was certain, was simple, attractive—and absolutely right.

The Sabras wanted to remain on Thalassa; they could do so. He did not doubt that they would become valuable citizens—perhaps exactly the aggressive, forceful type that this society needed.

How strange that History was repeating itself; like Magellan, he would be marooning some of his men.

But whether he had punished them or rewarded them, he would not know for three hundred years.

VI. THE FORESTS OF THE SEA

44. SPYBALL

The North Island Marine Lab had been less than enthusiastic.

"We still need a week to repair *Calypso*," the director said, "and we were lucky to find the sledge. It's the only one on Thalassa, and we don't want to risk it again."

I know the symptoms, thought Science Officer Varley; even during the last days on Earth, there were still some lab directors who wanted to keep their beautiful equipment unsullied by actual use.

"Unless Krakan Junior—or Senior—misbehaves again, I don't see that there's any risk. And haven't the geologists promised that they'll be quiet again for at least fifty years?"

"I've a small bet with them on *that*. But frankly—why do you think this is so important?"

What tunnel vision! Varley thought. Even if the man *is* a physical oceanographer, one would have expected him to have some interest in marine life. But perhaps I've misjudged him; he may be sounding me out . . .

"We have a certain emotional interest in the subject since Dr. Lorenson was killed—luckily not permanently. But quite apart from that, we find the scorps fascinating. *Anything* we can discover about alien intelligence could be of vital importance someday. And to *you* even more than to us since they're on your doorstep."

"I can appreciate that. Perhaps it's lucky we occupy such different ecological niches."

For how long? the science officer thought. If Moses Kaldor is right . . .

195

"Tell me just what a spyball does. The name's certainly intriguing."

"They were developed a couple of thousand years ago for security and espionage but had many other applications. Some weren't much bigger than pinheads—the one we'll use is the size of a football."

Varley spread the drawings on the director's table.

"This one was designed especially for underwater use—I'm surprised you're not familiar with it—the reference date is as early as 2045. We found complete specifications in Tech Memory, and fed them into the replicator. The first copy wouldn't work—we still don't know why—but number two tests out fine.

"Here are the acoustic generators—ten megahertz—so we've got millimeter resolution. Hardly video quality, of course, but good enough.

"The signal-processor is quite intelligent. When the spyball's switched on, it sends out a single pulse which builds up an acoustical hologram of everything within twenty or thirty meters. It transmits this information on a two-hundred-kilohertz narrow-band to the buoy floating topside, which radios it back to base. The first image takes ten seconds to build up; then the spyball pulses again.

"If there's no change in the picture, it sends a null signal. But if something happens, it transmits the new information so that an updated image can be generated.

"What we get, then, is a snapshot every ten seconds, which is good enough for most purposes. Of course, if things happen quickly, there will be bad image smearing. But you can't have everything; the system will work anywhere, in total darkness—it isn't easy to spot—and it's economical."

The director was obviously interested and was doing his best to keep his enthusiasm from showing.

"It's a clever toy—may be useful for our work. Can you give us the specs—and a few more models?"

"The specs—certainly, and we'll check that they interface with your replicator so you can make as many copies as you like. The first working model—and maybe the next two or three—we want to dump on Scorpville.

"And then we'll just wait and see what happens."

45. BAIT

The image was grainy, and sometimes hard to interpret despite the false-color coding that revealed details the eye could not otherwise detect. It was a flattened-out 360-degree panorama of seabed, with a distant view of kelp on the left, a few rock outcroppings at center, and kelp again on the right. Though it looked like a still photograph, the changing numbers at the lower left-hand corner revealed the passage of time; and occasionally the scene changed with a sudden jerk when some movement altered the information pattern being transmitted.

"As you'll see," Commander Varley told the invited audience in the Terra Nova auditorium, "there were no scorps around when we arrived, but they may have heard—or felt—the bump when our, ah, package landed. Here's the first investigator, at one minute, twenty seconds."

Now the image was changing abruptly at every ten-second interval, and more scorps were appearing in each frame.

"I'll freeze this one," said the science officer, "so that you can study the details. See that scorp on the right? Look at his left claw—no less than five of those metal bands! And he seems to be in a position of authority—in the next frames the other scorps have moved out of his way—now he's examining the mysterious pile of junk that's just fallen out of his sky—this is a particularly good shot—see how he uses claws and mouth palps together—one set for power, the other for precision—now he's pulling at the wire, but our little gift is too heavy to move—look at his attitude—I'll swear he's giving

198

orders, though we haven't detected any signal—maybe it's subsonic—here comes another of the big fellows—"

The scene shifted abruptly, tilting at a crazy angle.

"Here we go; they're dragging us along—and you were right, Dr. Kaldor—they're heading for that cave in the rock pyramid—the package is too big to go inside—just the way we planned it, of course—*this* is the really interesting part—"

A good deal of thought had gone into the present for the scorps. Although it consisted mostly of junk, that junk had been carefully selected. There were bars of steel, copper, aluminum, and lead; wooden planks; tubes and sheets of plastic; pieces of iron chain; a metal mirror—and several coils of copper wire of assorted gauges. The entire mass weighed over a hundred kilograms and had been carefully fastened together so that it could only be moved as a single unit. The spyball nestled inconspicuously at one corner, attached by four separate short cables.

The two big scorps were now attacking the pile of junk with determination and, it seemed, a definite plan. Their powerful claws quickly disposed of the wires holding it together, and they immediately discarded the pieces of wood and plastic; it was obvious that they were only interested in the metal.

The mirror gave them pause. They held it up and stared at their reflections—invisible, of course, in the spyball's acoustical image.

"We rather expected them to attack—you can start a good fight by putting a mirror in a tank of fish. Perhaps they recognize themselves. That seems to indicate a fair level of intelligence."

The scorps abandoned the mirror and began to drag the rest of the debris across the seabed. For the next few frames, the views were hopelessly confused. When the image stabilized again, it showed a completely different scene.

"We were in luck—things worked out exactly as we'd hoped. They've dragged the spyball into that guarded cave.

But it isn't the Queen Scorp's throne room—if there *is* a Queen Scorp, which I very much doubt . . . Theories, anyone?"

There was silence for a long time while the audience studied the strange spectacle. Then someone remarked, "It's a junk room!"

"But it must have a purpose—"

"Look—that's a ten-kilowatt outboard motor—someone must have dropped it!"

"Now we know who's been stealing our anchor chains!"

"But *why*—it doesn't make sense."

"Obviously it does—to them."

Moses Kaldor gave his attention-demanding cough, which seldom failed to work.

"This is still only a theory," he began, "but more and more the facts seem to support it. You'll notice that everything here is metal, carefully collected from a wide variety of sources . . .

"Now, to an intelligent marine creature, metal would be very mysterious, something quite different from all the other natural products of the ocean. The scorps seem to be still in the Stone Age—and there's no way they can get out of it as we land animals did on Earth. Without fire, they are trapped in a technological cul-de-sac.

"I think we may be seeing a replay of something that happened long ago on our own world. Do you know where prehistoric man got his first supplies of iron? From space!

"I don't blame you for looking surprised. But pure iron never occurs in nature—it rusts too easily. Primitive man's only source of supply was meteorites. No wonder they were worshiped; no wonder our ancestors believed in supernatural beings beyond the sky . . .

"Is the same story happening here? I urge you to consider it seriously. We still don't know the level of intelligence of the scorps. Perhaps they are collecting metals out of mere curiosity and fascination with their—shall I say magical?—properties. But will they discover how to use them for anything more

200

than decoration? How far can they progress—while they stay underwater? *Will* they stay there?

"My friends, I think you should learn all you possibly can about the scorps. You may be sharing your planet with another intelligent race. Are you going to cooperate or fight? Even if they are not really intelligent, the scorps could be a deadly menace—or a useful tool. Perhaps you should cultivate them. By the way, look up the reference Cargo Cult in your History Banks . . . that's C-A-R-G-O C-U-L-T.

"I would love to know the next chapter in this story. Are there scorp philosophers, even now, gathering in the kelp forests—to consider what to do about us?

"So *please*, repair the deep-space antenna so we can keep in touch! *Magellan's* computer will be waiting for your report— as it watches over us on the road to Sagan Two."

46. WHATEVER GODS MAY BE . . .

"What is God?" Mirissa asked.

Kaldor sighed and looked up from the centuries-old display he was scanning.

"Oh, dear. Why do you ask?"

"Because Loren said yesterday, 'Moses thinks the scorps may be looking for God.'"

"Did he indeed? I'll speak to him later. And you, young lady, are asking me to explain something that has obsessed millions of men for thousands of years and generated more words than any other single subject in history. How much time can you spare this morning?"

Mirissa laughed. "Oh, at least an hour. Didn't you once tell me that anything really important can be expressed in a single sentence?"

"Umm. Well, I've come across some exceedingly long-winded sentences in my time. Now, where shall I start . . ."

He let his eyes wander to the glade outside the library window and the silent—yet so eloquent!—hulk of the Mother Ship looming above it. Here human life began on this planet; no wonder it often reminds me of Eden. And am I the Snake, about to destroy its innocence? But I won't be telling a girl as clever as Mirissa anything that she doesn't already know—or guess.

"The trouble with the word God," he began slowly, "is that it never meant the same thing to any two people—especially if they were philosophers. That's why it slowly dropped out of use during the Third Millennium except as an expletive—in some cultures, too obscene for polite use.

202

"Instead, it was replaced by a whole constellation of specialized words. This at least stopped people arguing at cross-purposes, which caused ninety percent of the trouble in the past.

"The Personal God, sometimes called God One, became Alpha. It was the hypothetical entity supposed to watch over the affairs of everyday life—every individual, every *animal!*—and to reward good and punish evil, usually in a vaguely described existence after death. You worshiped Alpha, prayed to it, carried out elaborate religious ceremonies, and built huge churches in its honor . . .

"Then there was the God who created the universe and might or might not have had anything to do with it since then. That was Omega. By the time they'd finished dissecting God, the philosophers had used up all the other twenty or so letters of the ancient Greek alphabet, but Alpha and Omega will do very nicely for this morning. I'd guess that not more than ten billion man-years were ever spent discussing them.

"Alpha was inextricably entangled with religion—and that was its downfall. It might still have been around right up to the destruction of the Earth if the myriads of competing religions had left each other alone. But they couldn't do that, because each claimed to possess the One and Only Truth. So they had to destroy their rivals—which meant, in effect, not only every other religion but dissenters inside their own faith.

"Of course, I'm grossly simplifying; good men and women often transcended their beliefs, and it's quite possible that religion was *essential* to early human societies. Without supernatural sanctions to restrain them, men might never have cooperated in anything larger than tribal units. Not until it became corrupted by power and privilege did religion become an essentially antisocial force, the great good it had done being eclipsed by greater evils.

"You've never heard, I hope, of the Inquisition, of Witch Hunts, of Jihads. Would you believe that even well into the Space Age there were nations in which children could be officially executed because their *parents* adhered to a heretical subset of the state's particular brand of Alpha? You look shocked, but these things—and worse—happened while our ancestors were beginning the exploration of the Solar System.

"Fortunately for mankind, Alpha faded out of the picture, more or less gracefully, in the early 2000s. It was killed by a fascinating development called statistical theology. How much time do I have left? Won't Bobby be getting impatient?"

Mirissa glanced out of the big picture window. The palomino was happily munching at the grass around the base of the Mother Ship, and was clearly perfectly content.

"He won't wander off—as long as there's something to eat here. What was statistical theology?"

"It was the final assault on the problem of Evil. What brought it to a head was the rise of a very eccentric cult—they called themselves Neo-Manichees, don't ask me to explain why—around 2050. Incidentally, it was the first 'orbital religion'; although all the other faiths had used communications satellites to spread their doctrines, the NMs relied on them exclusively. They had no meeting place except the television screen.

"Despite this dependence on technology, their tradition was actually very old. They believed that Alpha existed but was completely *evil*—and that mankind's ultimate destiny was to confront and destroy it.

"In support of their faith, they marshaled an immense array of horrible facts from history and zoology. I think they must have been rather sick people, because they seemed to take a morbid delight in collecting such material.

"For example—a favorite proof of Alpha's existence was what's called the Argument from Design. We now know it's utterly fallacious, but the NMs made it sound totally convincing and irrefutable.

"If you find a beautifully designed system—their favorite example was a digital watch—then there must be a planner, a creator, behind it. So just look at the world of Nature—

"And they did, with a vengeance. Their special field was parasitology—you don't know how lucky you are on Thalassa, by the way! I won't revolt you by describing the incredibly ingenious methods and adaptations that various creatures used to invade other organisms—humans especially—and to prey on them, often until they were destroyed. I'll only mention one special pet of the NMs, the ichneumon fly.

"This delightful creature laid its eggs in other insects, after first paralyzing them, so that when their larvae hatched out, they would have an ample supply of fresh—*living*—meat.

"The NMs could go on for hours along these lines, expounding the wonders of Nature as proof that Alpha was, if not supremely evil, then utterly indifferent to human standards of morality and goodness. Don't worry—I can't imitate them, and won't.

"But I must mention another of their favorite proofs—the Argument from Catastrophe. A typical example, which could be multiplied countless times: Alpha worshipers gather to appeal for help in the face of disaster—and are all killed by the collapse of their refuge, whereas most of them would have been saved had they stayed at home.

"Again, the NMs collected volumes of such horrors—burning hospitals and old people's homes, infant schools engulfed by earthquakes, volcanoes, or tidal waves destroying cities—the list is endless.

"Of course, rival Alpha worshipers didn't take this lying down. *They* collected equal numbers of counterexamples—the wonderful things that had happened, time and again, to *save* devout believers from catastrophe.

"In various forms, this debate had been going on for several thousand years. But by the twenty-first century, the new information technologies and methods of statistical analysis as well as a wider understanding of probability theory allowed it to be settled.

"It took a few decades for the answers to come in, and a

205

few more before they were accepted by virtually all intelligent men: Bad things happened just as often as good; as had long been suspected, the universe simply obeyed the laws of mathematical probability. Certainly there was no sign of any supernatural intervention, either for good or for ill.

"So the problem of Evil never really existed. To expect the universe to be benevolent was like imagining one could *always* win at a game of pure chance.

"Some cultists tried to save the day by proclaiming the religion of Alpha the Utterly Indifferent and used the bell-shaped curve of normal distribution as the symbol of their faith. Needless to say, so abstract a deity didn't inspire much devotion.

"And while we're on the subject of mathematics, it gave Alpha another devastating blow in the twenty-first (or was it the twenty-second?) century. A brilliant Terran named Kurt Gödel proved that there were certain absolutely fundamental limits to knowledge, and hence the idea of a completely Omniscient Being—one of the definitions of Alpha—was logically absurd. This discovery has come down to us in one of those unforgettable bad puns: 'Gödel Deleted God.' Students used to write graffiti on walls with the letters G, O, and the Greek Delta; and of course there were versions that read: 'God Deleted Gödel'.

"But back to Alpha. By mid-millennium, it had more or less faded from human concerns. Virtually all thinking men had finally come to agree with the harsh verdict of the great philosopher Lucretius: *all* religions were fundamentally immoral, because the superstitions they peddled wrought more evil than good.

"Yet a few of the old faiths managed to survive, though in drastically altered forms, right up to the end of the Earth. The Latter Day Mormons and the Daughters of the Prophet even managed to build seedships of their own. I often wonder what happened to them.

"With Alpha discredited, that left Omega, the Creator of

everything. It's not so easy to dispose of Omega; the universe takes a certain amount of explaining. Or does it? There's an ancient philosophical joke that's much subtler than it seems. Question: Why is the Universe here? Answer: Where else would it be? And I think *that's* quite enough for one morning."

"Thank you, Moses," Mirissa answered, looking slightly dazed. "You've said all this before, haven't you?"

"Of course I have—many times. And promise me this—"

"What is it?"

"Don't believe *anything* I've told you—merely because I said it. No serious philosophical problem is ever settled. Omega is still around—and sometimes I wonder about Alpha . . ."

VII. AS THE SPARKS FLY UPWARD

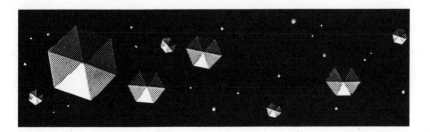

47. ASCENSION

Her name was Carina; she was eighteen years old, and though this was the first time she had ever been out at night in Kumar's boat, it was not by any means the first time she had lain in his arms. She had, indeed, perhaps the best title to the much-disputed claim of being his favorite girl.

Though the sun had set two hours ago, the inner moon—so much brighter and closer than the lost Moon of Earth—was almost full, and the beach, half a kilometer away, was awash with its cold, blue light. A small fire was burning just outside the line of the palm-trees, where the party was still in progress. And the faint sound of music could be heard from time to time above the gentle murmur of the jet drive operating at its very lowest power. Kumar had already arrived at his prime goal and was in no great hurry to go elsewhere. Nevertheless, like the good seaman he was, he occasionally disengaged himself to speak a few words of instruction to the autopilot and made a swift scan of the horizon.

Kumar had spoken the truth, thought Carina blissfully. There was something very erotic about the regular, gentle rhythm of a boat, especially when it was amplified by the airbed on which they were lying. After *this*, would she ever be satisfied by lovemaking on dry land?

And Kumar, unlike quite a few other young Tarnans she could mention, was surprisingly tender and considerate. He was not one of those men who was only concerned with his own satisfaction; his pleasure was not complete unless it was shared. While he's in me, Carina thought, I feel I'm the only

211

girl in his universe—even though I know perfectly well that isn't true.

Carina was vaguely aware that they were still heading away from the village, but she did not mind. She wished that this moment could last forever and would hardly have cared if the boat had been driving at full speed out into the empty ocean, with no land ahead until the circumnavigation of the globe. Kumar knew what he was doing—in more ways than one. Part of her pleasure derived from the utter confidence he inspired; within his arms, she had no worries, no problems. The future did not exist; there was only the timeless present.

Yet time did pass, and now the inner moon was much higher in the sky. In the aftermath of passion, their lips were still languidly exploring the territories of love when the pulsing of the hydrojet ceased and the boat drifted to a stop.

"We're here," Kumar said, a note of excitement in his voice.

And where may "here" be? Carina thought lazily as they rolled apart. It seemed hours since she had last bothered to glance at the coastline . . . even assuming that it was still within sight.

She climbed slowly to her feet, steadying herself against the gentle rocking of the boat—and stared wide-eyed at the Fairyland that, not long ago, had been the dismal swamp hopefully but inaccurately christened Mangrove Bay.

It was not, of course, the first time she had encountered high technology; the fusion plant and Main Replicator on North Island were much larger and more impressive. But to see this brilliantly illuminated labyrinth of pipes and storage tanks and cranes and handling mechanisms—this bustling combination of shipyard and chemical plant, all functioning silently and efficiently under the stars with not a single human being in sight—was a real visual and psychological shock.

There was a sudden splash, startling in the utter silence of the night, as Kumar threw out the anchor.

"Come on," he said mischievously. "I want to show you something."

"Is it safe?"

"Of course—I've been here lots of times."

And not by yourself, I'm sure, Carina thought. But he was already over the side before she could make any comment.

The water was barely more than waist deep and still retained so much of the day's heat that it was almost uncomfortably warm. When Carina and Kumar walked up on to the beach, hand in hand, it was refreshing to feel the cool night breeze against their bodies. They emerged from the random rippling of tiny wavelets like a new Adam and Eve given the keys to a mechanized Eden.

"Don't worry!" Kumar said. "I know my way around. Dr. Lorenson's explained everything to me. But I've found something I'm sure *he* doesn't know."

They were walking along a line of heavily insulated pipes, supported a meter from the ground, and now for the first time Carina could hear a distinct sound—the throbbing of pumps forcing cooling fluid through the maze of plumbing and heat exchangers that surrounded them.

Presently they came to the famous tank in which the scorp had been found. Very little water was now visible; the surface was almost completely covered with a tangled mass of kelp. There were no reptiles on Thalassa, but the thick, flexible stalks reminded Carina of intertwining snakes.

They walked along a series of culverts and past small sluice gates, all of them closed at the moment, until they reached a wide, open area, well away from the main plant. As they left the central complex, Kumar waved cheerfully at the lens of a pointing camera. No one ever discovered, later, why it had been switched off at the crucial moment.

"The freezing tanks," Kumar said. "Six hundred tons in each. Ninety-five percent water, five percent kelp. What's so funny?"

"Not funny—but very *strange*," answered Carina, still smiling. "Just think of it—carrying some of our ocean forest all

213

the way to the stars. Who would ever imagine such a thing! But *that's* not why you brought me here."

"No," said Kumar softly. "Look . . ."

At first, she could not see what he was pointing at. Then her mind interpreted the image that flickered at the very edge of vision, and she understood.

It was an old miracle, of course. Men had done such things on many worlds for over a thousand years. But to witness it with her own eyes was more than breathtaking—it was awesome.

Now that they had walked closer to the last of the tanks, she could see it more clearly. The thin thread of light—it could not have been more than a couple of centimeters wide!—climbed upward to the stars, straight and true as a laser beam. Her eyes followed it until it narrowed into invisibility, teasing her to decide the exact place of its disappearance. And still her gaze swept onward, dizzyingly, until she was staring at the zenith itself and at the single star that was poised motionless there while all its fainter, natural companions marched steadily past it toward the west. Like some cosmic spider, *Magellan* had lowerd a thread of gossamer and would soon be hoisting the prize it desired from the world below.

Now that they were standing at the very edge of the waiting ice block, Carina had another surprise. Its surface was completely covered with a glittering layer of golden foil, reminding her of the gifts that were presented to children on their birthdays or at the annual Landing Festival.

"Insulation," Kumar explained. "And it really *is* gold—about two atoms thick. Without it, half the ice would melt again before it could get up to the shield."

Insulation or no, Carina could feel the bite of cold through her bare feet as Kumar led her out on to the frozen slab. They reached its center in a dozen steps—and there, glittering with a curious nonmetallic sheen, was the taut ribbon that stretched, if not to the stars, at least the thirty thousand kilo-

214

meters up to the stationary orbit in which *Magellan* was now parked.

It ended in a cylindrical drum, studded with instruments and control jets, which clearly served as a mobile, intelligent crane-hook, homing on to its load after its long descent through the atmosphere. The whole arrangement looked surprisingly simple and even unsophisticated—deceptively so, like most products of mature, advanced technologies.

Carina suddenly shivered, and not from the cold underfoot, which she now scarcely noticed.

"Are you sure it's safe here?" she asked anxiously.

"Of course. They always lift at midnight, on the second— and that's still hours away. It's a wonderful sight, but I don't think we'll stay so late."

Now Kumar was kneeling, placing his ear against the incredible ribbon that bound ship and planet together. If it snapped, she wondered anxiously, would they fly apart?

"Listen," he whispered . . .

She had not known what to expect. Sometimes in later years, when she could endure it, she tried to recapture the magic of this moment. She could never be sure if she had succeeded.

At first it seemed that she was hearing the deepest note of a giant harp whose strings were stretched between the worlds. It sent shivers down her spine, and she felt the little hairs at the nape of her neck stirring in that immemorial fear response forged in the primeval jungles of Earth.

Then, as she grew accustomed to it, she became aware of a whole spectrum of shifting overtones covering the range of hearing to the very limits of audibility—and doubtless far beyond. They blurred and merged one into the other, as inconstant, yet steadily repeating, as the sounds of the sea.

The more she listened, the more she was reminded of the endless beating of the waves upon a desolate beach. She felt that she was hearing the sea of space wash upon the shores of all its worlds—a sound terrifying in its meaningless futility

215

as it reverberated through the aching emptiness of the universe.

And now she became aware of other elements in this immensely complex symphony. There were sudden, plangent twangings, as if giant fingers had plucked at the ribbon somewhere along its thousands of taut kilometers. Meteorites? Surely not. Perhaps some electrical discharge in Thalassa's seething ionosphere? And—was this pure imagination, something created by her own unconscious fears?—it seemed that from time to time she heard the faint wailing of demon voices or the ghostly cries of all the sick and starving children who had died on Earth during the Nightmare Centuries.

Suddenly, she could bear it no longer.

"I'm frightened, Kumar," she whispered, tugging at his shoulder. "Let's go."

But Kumar was still lost in the stars, his mouth half open as he pressed his head against that resonant ribbon, hypnotized by its siren song. He never even noticed when, angry as much as scared, Carina stomped across the foil-covered ice and stood waiting for him on the familiar warmth of dry land.

For now he had noticed something new—a series of rising notes that seemed to be calling for his attention. It was like a Fanfare for Strings, if one could imagine such a thing, and it was ineffably sad and distant.

But it was coming closer, growing louder. It was the most thrilling sound that Kumar had ever heard, and it held him paralyzed with astonishment and awe. He could almost imagine that *something* was racing down the ribbon toward him . . .

Seconds too late, he realized the truth as the first shock of the precursor wave jolted him flat against the golden foil and the ice block stirred beneath him. Then, for the very last time, Kumar Leonidas looked upon the fragile beauty of his sleeping world and the terrified, upturned face of the girl who would remember this moment until her own dying day.

Already, it was too late to jump. And so the Little Lion ascended to the silent stars—naked and alone.

48. DECISION

Captain Bey had graver problems on his mind and was very glad to delegate this task. In any event, no emissary could have been more appropriate than Loren Lorenson.

He had never met the Leonidas elders before and dreaded the encounter. Though Mirissa had offered to accompany him, he preferred to go alone.

The Lassans revered their old folk and did everything possible for their comfort and happiness. Lal and Nikri Leonidas lived in one of the small, self-contained retirement colonies along the south coast of the island. They had a six-room chalet with every conceivable labor-saving device, including the only general-purpose house robot that Loren had ever seen on South Island. By Earth chronology, he would have judged them to be in their late sixties.

After the initial subdued greetings, they sat on the porch, looking out to the sea while the robot fussed around bearing drinks and plates of assorted fruit. Loren forced himself to eat a few morsels, then gathered his courage and tackled the hardest task of his life.

"Kumar—" The name stuck in his throat, and he had to begin again. "Kumar is still on the ship. I owe my life to him; he risked his to save mine. You can understand how I feel about this—I would do *anything* . . ."

Once more he had to fight for control. Then, trying to be as brisk and scientific as he could—like Surgeon Commander Newton during her briefing—he made yet another start.

"His body is almost undamaged, because decompression was slow and freezing took place immediately. But, of course,

217

he is clinically dead—just as I was myself a few weeks ago . . .

"However, the two cases are very different. My—body— was recovered before there was time for brain damage, so revival was a fairly straightforward process.

"It was hours before they recovered Kumar. Physically, his brain is undamaged—but there is no trace of any activity.

"Even so, revival *may* be possible with extremely advanced technology. According to our records—which cover the entire history of Earth's medical science—it has been done before in similar cases, with a success rate of sixty percent.

"And that places us in a dilemma, which Captain Bey has asked me to explain to you frankly. We do not have the skills or the equipment to carry out such an operation. But we may—in three hundred year's time . . .

"There are a dozen brain experts among the hundreds of medical specialists sleeping aboard the ship. There are technicians who can assemble and operate every conceivable type of surgical and life-support gear. All that Earth ever possessed will be ours again—soon after we reach Sagan Two . . ."

He paused to let the implications sink in. The robot took this inopportune moment to offer its services; he waved it away.

"We would be willing—no, glad, for it is the very least we can do—to take Kumar with us. Though we cannot guarantee it, one day he may live again. We would like you to think it over; there is plenty of time before you have to make the decision."

The old couple looked at each other for a long, silent moment while Loren stared out to sea. How quiet and peaceful it was! He would be glad to spend his own declining years here, visited from time to time by children and grandchildren . . .

Like so much of Tarna, it might almost be Earth. Perhaps through deliberate planning, there was no Lassan vegetation anywhere in sight; all the trees were hauntingly familiar.

Yet something essential was lacking; he realized that it had been puzzling him for a long time—indeed, ever since he had landed on this planet. And suddenly, as if this moment of grief had triggered the memory, he knew what he had missed.

There were no sea gulls wheeling in the sky, filling the air with the saddest and most evocative of all the sounds of Earth.

Lal Leonidas and his wife had still not exchanged a word, yet somehow Loren knew that they had made their decision.

"We appreciate your offer, Commander Lorenson; please express our thanks to Captain Bey.

"But we do not need any time to consider it. Whatever happens, Kumar will be lost to us forever.

"Even if you succeed—and as you say, there is no guarantee—he will awaken in a strange world, knowing that he will never see his home again and that all those he loved are centuries dead. It does not bear thinking of. You mean well, but that would be no kindness to him.

"We know what he would have wished and what must be done. Give him back to us. We will return him to the sea he loved."

There was nothing more to be said. Loren felt both an overwhelming sadness and a vast relief.

He had done his duty. It was the decision he had expected.

49. FIRE ON THE REEF

Now the little kayak would never be completed; but it would make its first and its last voyage.

Until sunset, it had lain at the water's edge, lapped by the gentle waves of the tideless sea. Loren was moved, but not surprised, to see how many had come to pay their last respects. All Tarna was here, but many had also come from all over South Island—and even from North. Though some, perhaps, had been drawn by morbid curiosity—for the whole world had been shocked by the uniquely spectacular accident— Loren had never seen such a genuine outpouring of grief. He had not realized that the Lassans were capable of such deep emotion, and in his mind he savored once again a phrase that Mirissa had found, searching the Archives for consolation: "Little friend of all the world." Its origin was lost, and no one could guess what long-dead scholar, in what century, had saved it for the ages to come.

Once he had embraced them both with wordless sympathy, he had left Mirissa and Brant with the Leonidas family, gathered with numerous relatives from both islands. He did not want to meet any strangers, for he knew what many of them must be thinking. "He saved you—but you could not save him." That was a burden he would carry for the rest of his life.

He bit his lip to check the tears that were not appropriate for a senior officer of the greatest starship ever built and felt one of the mind's defense mechanisms come to his rescue. At moments of deep grief, sometimes the only way to prevent loss of control is to evoke some wholly incongruous—even comic—image from the depths of memory.

Yes—the universe had a strange sense of humor. Loren was almost forced to suppress a smile; how Kumar would have enjoyed the final joke it had played on him!

"Don't be surprised," Commander Newton had warned as she opened the door of the ship's morgue and a gust of icy, formalin-tainted air rolled out to meet them. "It happens more often than you think. Sometimes it's a final spasm—almost like an unconscious attempt to defy Death. This time, it was probably caused by the loss of external pressure and the subsequent freezing."

Had it not been for the crystals of ice defining the muscles of the splendid young body, Loren might have thought that Kumar was not merely sleeping, but lost in blissful dreams.

For in death, the Little Lion was even more male than he had been in life.

And now the sun had vanished behind the low hills to the west, and a cool evening breeze was rising from the sea. With scarcely a ripple, the kayak slipped into the water, drawn by Brant and three other of Kumar's closest friends. For the last time Loren glimpsed the calm and peaceful face of the boy to whom he owed his life.

There had been little weeping until now, but as the four swimmers pushed the boat slowly out from the shore, a great wail of lamentation rose from the assembled crowd. Now Loren could no longer contain his tears and did not care who saw them.

Moving strongly and steadily under the powerful drive of its four escorts, the little kayak headed out to the reef. The quick Thalassan night was already descending as the craft passed between the two flashing beacons that marked the channel to the open sea. It vanished beyond them, and for a moment was hidden by the white line of breakers foaming lazily against the outer reef.

The lamentation ceased; everyone was waiting. Then there was a sudden flare of light against the darkling sky, and a pillar of fire rose out of the sea. It burned cleanly and fiercely, with scarcely any smoke; how long it lasted, Loren never knew, for time had ceased on Tarna.

Then, abruptly, the flames collapsed; the crown of fire shrank back into the sea. All was darkness; but for a moment only.

As fire and water met, a fountain of sparks erupted into the sky. Most of the embers fell back upon the sea, but others continued to soar upward until they were lost from view.

And so, for the second time, Kumar Leonidas ascended to the stars.

VIII. THE SONGS OF DISTANT EARTH

50. SHIELD OF ICE

The lifting of the last snowflake should have been a joyful occasion; now it was merely one of somber satisfaction. Thirty thousand kilometers above Thalassa, the final hexagon of ice was jockeyed into position, and the shield was complete.

For the first time in almost two years, the quantum drive was activated, though at minimum power. *Magellan* broke away from its stationary orbit, accelerating to test the balance and the integrity of the artificial iceberg it was to carry out to the stars. There were no problems; the work had been well done. This was a great relief to Captain Bey, who had never been able to forget that Owen Fletcher (now under reasonably strict surveillance on North Island) had been one of the shield's principal architects. And he wondered what Fletcher and the other exiled Sabras had thought when they watched the dedication ceremony.

It had begun with a video retrospective showing the building of the freezing plant and the lifting of the first snowflake. Then there had been a fascinating, speeded-up space ballet showing the great blocks of ice being maneuvered into place and keyed into the steadily growing shield. It had started in real time, then rapidly accelerated until the last sections were being added at the rate of one every few seconds. Thalassa's leading composer had contrived a witty musical score beginning with a slow pavane and culminating in a breathless polka—slowing down to normal speed again at the very end as the final block of ice was jockeyed into position.

Then the view had switched to a live camera hovering in space a kilometer ahead of *Magellan* as it orbited in the shadow

225

of the planet. The big sun-screen that protected the ice during the day had been moved aside, so the entire shield was now visible for the first time.

The huge greenish-white disc gleamed coldly beneath the floodlights; soon it would be far colder as it moved out into the few-degrees-above-absolute zero of the galactic night. There it would be warmed only by the background light of the stars, the radiation leakage from the ship—and the occasional rare burst of energy from impacting dust.

The camera drifted slowly across the artificial iceberg, to the accompaniment of Moses Kaldor's unmistakable voice.

"People of Thalassa, we thank you for your gift. Behind this shield of ice, we hope to travel safely to the world that is waiting for us, seventy-five light-years away, three hundred years hence.

"If all goes well, we will still be carrying at least twenty thousand tons of ice when we reach Sagan Two. That will be allowed to fall on to the planet, and the heat of reentry will turn it into the first rain that frigid world has ever known. For a little while, before it freezes again, it will be the precursor of oceans yet unborn.

"And one day our descendants will know seas like yours, though not as wide or as deep. Water from our two worlds will mingle together, bringing life to our new home. And we will remember you with love and gratitude."

51. RELIC

"It's beautiful," Mirissa said reverently. "I can understand why gold was so prized on Earth."

"The gold is the least important part," Kaldor answered as he slid the gleaming bell out of its velvet-lined box. "Can you guess what this is?"

"It's obviously a work of art. But it must be something much more for you to have carried it across fifty light-years."

"You're right, of course. It's an exact model of a great temple, more than a hundred meters tall. Originally, there were seven of these caskets, all identical in shape, nesting one inside the other—this was the innermost, holding the Relic itself. It was given to me by some old and dear friends on my very last night on Earth. 'All things are impermanent,' they reminded me. 'But we have guarded this for more than four thousand years. Take it with you to the stars, with our blessings.'

"Even though I did not share their faith, how could I refuse so priceless an offering? And now I will leave it here, where men first came to this planet—another gift from Earth—perhaps the last."

"Don't say that," Mirissa said. "You have left so many gifts—we will never be able to count them all."

Kaldor smiled wistfully and did not answer for a moment as he let his eyes linger on the familiar view from the library window. He had been happy here, tracing the history of Thalassa and learning much that might be of priceless value when the new colony was started on Sagan Two.

Farewell, old Mother Ship, he thought. You did your work

well. We still have far to go; may *Magellan* serve us as faithfully as you served the people we have grown to love.

"I'm sure my friends would have approved—I've done my duty. The Relic will be safer here, in the Museum of Earth, than aboard the ship. After all, we may never reach Sagan Two."

"Of course you will. But you haven't told me what's inside this seventh casket."

"It's all that's left of one of the greatest men who ever lived; he founded the only faith that never became stained with blood. I'm sure he would have been most amused to know that, forty centuries after his death, one of his teeth would be carried to the stars."

52. THE SONGS OF DISTANT EARTH

Now was a time of transition, of farewells—of partings as deep as death. Yet for all the tears that were shed—on Thalassa as well as the ship—there was also a feeling of relief. Though things would never be quite the same again, life could now return to normal. The visitors were like guests who had slightly overstayed their welcome; it was time to go.

Even President Farradine now accepted this and had abandoned his dream of an interstellar Olympics. He had ample consolation; the freezing units at Mangrove Bay were being transferred to North Island, and the first skating rink on Thalassa would be ready in time for the Games. Whether any competitors would also be ready was another question, but many young Lassans were spending hours staring incredulously at some of the great performers of the past.

Meanwhile, everyone agreed that some farewell ceremony should be arranged to mark *Magellan*'s departure. Unfortunately, few could agree what form it should take. There were innumerable private parties—which put a considerable mental and physical strain on all concerned—but no official, public one.

Mayor Waldron, claiming priority on behalf of Tarna, felt that the ceremony should take place at First Landing. Edgar Farradine argued that the President's Palace, despite its modest size, was more appropriate. Some wit suggested Krakan as a compromise, pointing out that its famous vineyards would be an appropriate place for the farewell toasts. The matter was still unresolved when the Thalassan Broadcasting

Corporation—one of the planet's more enterprising bureau-
cracies—quietly preempted the entire project.

The farewell concert was to be remembered, and replayed,
for generations to come. There was no video to distract the
senses—only music and the briefest of narration. The heritage
of two thousand years was ransacked to recall the past and
to give hope for the future. It was not only a Requiem but
also a Berceuse.

It still seemed a miracle that after their art had reached technological perfection, composers of music could find anything
new to say. For two thousand years, electronics had given
them complete command over every sound audible to the
human ear, and it might have been thought that all the possibilities of the medium had been long exhausted.

There had, indeed, been about a century of beepings and
twitterings and electroeructations before composers had mastered their now infinite powers and had once again successfully married technology and art. No one had ever surpassed
Beethoven or Bach; but some had approached them.

To the legions of listeners, the concert was a reminder of
things they had never known—things that belonged to Earth
alone. The slow beat of mighty bells, climbing like invisible
smoke from old cathedral spires; the chant of patient boatmen,
in tongues now lost forever, rowing home against the tide in
the last light of day; the songs of armies marching into battles
that Time had robbed of all their pain and evil; the merged
murmur of ten million voices as man's greatest cities awoke
to meet the dawn; the cold dance of the aurora over endless
seas of ice; the roar of mighty engines climbing upward on
the highway to the stars. All these the listeners heard in the
music that came out of the night—the songs of distant Earth,
carried across the light-years . . .

For the concluding item, the producers had selected the last
great work in the symphonic tradition. Written in the years
when Thalassa had lost touch with Earth, it was totally new
to the audience. Yet its oceanic theme made it peculiarly ap-

230

propriate to this occasion—and its impact upon the listeners was everything the long-dead composer could have wished.

". . . When I wrote the 'Lamentation for Atlantis,' almost thirty years ago, I had no specific images in mind; I was concerned only with emotional reactions, not explicit scenes; I wanted the music to convey a sense of mystery, of sadness— of overwhelming loss. I was not trying to paint a sound-portrait of ruined cities full of fish. But now something strange happens whenever I hear the *Lento lugubre*—as I am doing in my mind at this very moment . . .

"It begins at Bar 136, when the series of chords descending to the organ's lowest register first meets the soprano's wordless aria, rising higher and higher out of the depths . . . You know, of course, that I based that theme on the songs of the great whales, those mighty minstrels of the sea with whom we made peace too late, too late . . . I wrote it for Olga Kondrashin, and no one else could ever sing those passages without electronic backing . . .

"When the vocal line begins, it's as if I'm seeing something that really exists. I'm standing in a great city square almost as large as St. Marks or St. Peters. All around are half-ruined buildings, like Greek temples, and overturned statues draped with seaweeds, green fronds waving slowly back and forth. Everything is partly covered by a thick layer of silt.

"The square seems empty at first; then I notice something— *disturbing*. Don't ask me why it's always a surprise, why I'm always seeing it for the first time . . .

"There's a low mound in the center of the square with a pattern of lines radiating from it. I wonder if they are ruined walls, partly buried in the silt. But the arrangement makes no sense; and then I see that the mound is—*pulsing*.

"And a moment later I notice two huge, unblinking eyes staring out at me.

"That's all; nothing happens. Nothing *has* happened here for six thousand years, since that night when the land barrier

231

gave way and the sea poured in through the Pillars of Hercules.

"The *Lento* is my favorite movement, but I couldn't end the symphony in such a mood of tragedy and despair. Hence the Finale, 'Resurgence.'

"I know, of course, that Plato's Atlantis never really existed. And for that very reason, it can never die. It will always be an ideal—a dream of perfection—a goal to inspire men for all ages to come. So that's why the symphony ends with a triumphant march into the future.

"I know that the popular interpretation of the march is a New Atlantis emerging from the waves. That's rather too literal; to me the finale depicts the conquest of space. Once I'd found it and pinned it down, it took me months to get rid of that closing theme. Those damned fifteen notes were hammering away in my brain night and day . . .

"Now, the *Lamentation* exists quite apart from me; it has taken on a life of its own. Even when Earth is gone, it will be speeding out toward the Andromeda Galaxy, driven by fifty thousand megawatts from the Deep Space transmitter in Tsiolkovski Crater.

"Someday, centuries or millennia hence, it will be captured—and understood."

Spoken Memoirs—Sergei Di Pietro (3411–3509)

53. THE GOLDEN MASK

"We've always pretended she doesn't exist," Mirissa said. "But now I would like to see her—just once."

Loren was silent for a while. Then he answered, "You know that Captain Bey has never allowed any visitors."

Of course she knew that; she also understood the reasons why. Although it had aroused some resentment at first, everyone on Thalassa now realized that *Magellan*'s small crew was far too busy to act as tour guides—or nursemaids—to the unpredictable fifteen percent who would become nauseated in the ship's zero-gravity sections. Even President Farradine had been tactfully turned down.

"I've spoken to Moses—and he's spoken to the captain. It's all arranged. But it's to be kept secret until the ship has left."

Loren stared at her in amazement; then he smiled. Mirissa was always surprising him; that was part of her attraction. And he realized, with a twinge of sadness, that no one on Thalassa had a better right to this privilege; her brother was the only other Lassan to have made the journey. Captain Bey was a fair man, willing to alter the rules when necessary. And once the ship had left, only three days from now, it would not matter.

"Suppose you're spacesick?"

"I've never even been seasick—"

"—that doesn't prove anything—"

"—and I've seen Commander Newton. She's given me a ninety-five percent rating. And she suggests the midnight

233

shuttle—there won't be any villagers around then."

"You've thought of everything, haven't you?" Loren said in frank admiration. "I'll meet you at Number Two Landing, fifteen minutes before midnight."

He paused, then added with difficulty, "I won't be coming down again. Please say good-bye to Brant for me."

That was an ordeal he could not face. Indeed, he had not set foot in the Leonidas residence since Kumar had made his last voyage and Brant had returned to comfort Mirissa. Already, it was almost as if Loren had never entered their lives.

And he was inexorably leaving theirs, for now he could look on Mirissa with love but without desire. A deeper emotion— one of the worst pains he had ever known—now filled his mind.

He had longed, and hoped, to see his child—but *Magellan*'s new schedule made that impossible. Though he had heard his son's heartbeats mingled with his mother's, he would never hold him in his arms.

The shuttle made its rendezvous on the day side of the planet, so *Magellan* was still almost a hundred kilometers away when Mirissa first saw it. Even though she knew its real size, it looked like a child's toy as it glittered in the sunlight.

From ten kilometers, it seemed no larger. Her brain and eyes insisted that those dark circles around the center section were only portholes. Not until the endless, curving hull of the ship loomed up beside them did her mind admit that they were cargo and docking hatches, one of which the ferry was about to enter.

Loren looked at Mirissa anxiously as she unbuckled her seatbelt; this was the dangerous moment when, free from restraints for the first time, the overconfident passenger suddenly realized that zero-gravity was not as enjoyable as it looked. But Mirissa seemed completely at ease as she drifted through the airlock, propelled by a few gentle pushes from Loren.

"Luckily there's no need to go into the one-gee section, so you'll avoid the problem of readapting twice. You won't have to worry about gravity again until you're back on the ground."

It would have been interesting, Mirissa thought, to have visited the living quarters in the spinning section of the ship—but that would have involved them in endless polite conversations and personal contacts, which were the last things she needed now. She was rather glad that Captain Bey was still down on Thalassa; there was no need even for a courtesy visit of thanks.

Once they had left the airlock they found themselves in a tubular corridor that seemed to stretch the whole length of the ship. On one side was a ladder; on the other, two lines of flexible loops, convenient for hands or feet, glided slowly in either direction along parallel slots.

"This is not a very good place to be when we're accelerating," Loren said. "Then it becomes a vertical shaft—two kilometers deep. That's when you *really* need the ladder and handholds. Just grab that loop and let it do all the work."

They were swept effortlessly along for several hundred meters, then switched to a corridor at right angles to the main one. "Let go of the strap," Loren said when they had traveled a few dozen meters. "I want to show you something."

Mirissa released her hold, and they drifted to a stop beside a long, narrow window set in the side of the tunnel. She peered through the thick glass into a huge, brightly lit metal cavern. Though she had quite lost her bearings, she guessed that this great cylindrical chamber must span almost the entire width of the ship—and that central bar must therefore lie along its axis.

"The quantum drive," Loren said proudly.

He did not even attempt to name the shrouded metal and crystal shapes, the curiously formed flying buttresses springing from the walls of the chamber, the pulsing constellations of lights, the sphere of utter blackness that even though it was completely featureless, somehow seemed to be spinning . . . But after a while he said:

"The greatest achievement of human genius—Earth's last gift to its children. One day it will make us masters of the galaxy."

There was an arrogance about the words that made Mirissa wince. That was the old Loren speaking again, before he had been mellowed by Thalassa. So be it, she thought; but part of him has been changed forever.

"Do you suppose," she asked gently, "that the galaxy will even notice?"

Yet she was impressed, and stared for a long time at the huge and meaningless shapes that had carried Loren to her across the light-years. She did not know whether to bless them for what they had brought her or to curse them for what they would soon take away.

Loren led her on through the maze, deeper into *Magellan's* heart. Not once did they meet another person; it was a reminder of the ship's size—and the smallness of its crew.

"We're nearly there," Loren said in a voice that was now hushed and solemn. "And *this* is the Guardian."

Taken completely by surprise, Mirissa floated toward the golden face staring at her out of the alcove until she was about to collide with it. She put out her hand and felt cold metal. So it was real—and not, as she had first imagined, a holodisplay.

"What—who—is it?" she whispered.

"We have many of Earth's greatest art treasures on board," Loren said with somber pride. "This was one of the most famous. He was a king who died very young—when he was still a boy . . ."

Loren's voice faded away as they shared the same thought. Mirissa had to blink away her tears before she could read the inscription below the mask.

TUTANKHAMEN
1361–1353 B.C.
(Valley of the Kings, Egypt, A.D. 1922)

Yes, he had been almost exactly the same age as Kumar. The golden face stared out at them across the millennia and across the light-years—the face of a young god struck down in his prime. There was power and confidence here, but not yet the arrogance and cruelty that the lost years would have given.

"Why here?" Mirissa asked, half guessing the answer.

"It seemed an appropriate symbol. The Egyptians believed that if they carried out the right ceremonies, the dead would exist again in some kind of afterworld. Pure superstition, of course—yet here we have made it come true."

But not in the way I would have wished, Mirissa thought sadly. As she stared into the jet-black eyes of the boy king, looking out at her from his mask of incorruptible gold, it was hard to believe that this was only a marvelous work of art and not a living person.

She could not tear her eyes away from that calm yet hypnotic gaze across the centuries. Once more she put forth her hand and stroked a golden cheek. The precious metal suddenly reminded her of a poem she had found in the First Landing Archives, when she set the computer searching the literature of the past for words of solace. Most of the hundreds of lines had been inappropriate, but this one ("Author unknown—?1800–2100") fitted perfectly:

> They carry back bright to the coiner the mintage of
> man,
> The lads that will die in their glory and never be old.

Loren waited patiently until Mirissa's thoughts had run their course. Then he slid a card into an almost invisible slot beside the death-mask, and a circular door opened silently.

237

It was incongruous to find a cloak-room full of heavy furs inside a spaceship, but Mirissa could appreciate the need for them. Already the temperature had fallen many degrees, and she found herself shivering with the unaccustomed cold.

Loren helped her into the thermosuit—not without difficulty in zero gravity—and they floated toward a circle of frosted glass set in the far wall of the little chamber. The crystal trapdoor swung toward them like an opening watchglass, and out of it swirled a blast of frigid air such as Mirissa had never imagined, far less experienced. Thin wisps of moisture condensed in the freezing air, dancing around her like ghosts. She looked at Loren as if to say, "Surely you don't expect me to go in *there!*"

He took her arm reassuringly and said, "Don't worry—the suit will protect you, and after a few minutes you won't notice the cold on your face."

She found this hard to believe; but he was right. As she followed him through the trapdoor, breathing cautiously at first, she was surprised to find the experience not at all unpleasant. Indeed, it was positively stimulating; for the first time she could understand why people had willingly gone into the polar regions of the Earth.

She could easily imagine that she was there herself, for she seemed to be floating in a frigid, snow-white universe. All around her were glittering honeycombs that might have been made of ice, forming thousands of hexagonal cells. It was almost like a smaller version of *Magellan*'s shield—except that here the units were only about a meter across and laced together with clusters of pipes and bundles of wiring.

So here they were, sleeping all around her—the hundreds of thousands of colonists to whom Earth was still, in literal truth, a memory of only yesterday. What were they dreaming, she wondered, less than halfway through their five-hundred-year sleep? Did the brain dream at all in this dim no-man's-land between life and death? Not according to Loren; but who could be really sure?

Mirissa had seen videos of bees scurrying about their mysterious business inside a hive; she felt like a human bee as she followed Loren, hand over hand along the grid-work of rails crisscrossing the face of the great honeycomb. She was now quite at ease in zero gravity and was no longer even aware of the bitter cold. Indeed, she was scarcely aware of her body and sometimes had to persuade herself that this was not all a dream from which she would presently awake.

The cells bore no names but were all identified by an alphanumeric code; Loren went unerringly to H-354. At the touch of a button, the hexagonal metal-and-glass container slid outward on telescopic rails to reveal the sleeping woman inside.

She was not beautiful—though it was unfair to pass judgment on any woman without the crowning glory of her hair. Her skin was of a color that Mirissa had never seen and which she knew had become very rare on Earth—a black so deep that it held almost a hint of blue. And it was so flawless that Mirissa could not resist a spasm of envy; into her mind came a fleeting image of intertwined bodies, ebon and ivory—an image that, she knew, would haunt her in the years ahead.

She looked again at the face. Even in this centuries-long repose, it showed determination and intelligence. Would we have been friends? Mirissa wondered. I doubt it; we are too much alike.

So you are Kitani, and you are carrying Loren's first child out to the stars. But will she really be the first, since she will be born centuries after mine? First or second, I wish her well . . .

She was still numb, though not only with cold, when the crystal door closed behind them. Loren steered her gently back along the corridor and past the Guardian.

Once more her fingers brushed the cheek of the immortal

239

ARTHUR C. CLARKE

golden boy. For a shocked moment, it felt warm to her touch; then she realized that her body was still adjusting to normal temperature.

That would take only minutes; but how long, she wondered, before the ice would melt around her heart?

54. VALEDICTION

This is the last time I shall talk to you, Evelyn, before I begin my longest sleep. I am still on Thalassa, but the shuttle will be lifting for *Magellan* in a few minutes; there is nothing more for me to do—until planetfall, three hundred years from now . . .

I feel a great sadness, for I have just said good-bye to my dearest friend here, Mirissa Leonidas. How you would have enjoyed meeting her! She is perhaps the most intelligent person I have met on Thalassa, and we had many long talks together—though I fear that some were more like the monologues for which you so often criticized me . . .

She asked about god, of course; but perhaps her shrewdest question was one I was quite unable to answer.

Soon after her beloved young brother was killed, she asked me, "What is the purpose of grief? Does it serve any biological function?"

How strange that I had never given any serious thought to that! One could imagine an intelligent species that functioned perfectly well if the dead were remembered with no emotion—if indeed they were remembered at all. It would be an utterly inhuman society, but it could be at least as successful as the termites and the ants were on Earth.

Could grief be an accidental—even a pathological—by-product of love, which of course *does* have an essential biological function? It's a strange and disturbing thought. Yet it's our emotions that make us human; who would abandon them, even knowing that each new love is yet another hostage to those twin terrorists, Time and Fate?

241

She often talked to me about you, Evelyn. It puzzled her that a man could love only one woman in all his life and not seek another when she was gone. Once I teased her by saying that fidelity was almost as strange to the Lassans as jealousy; she retorted that they had gained by losing both.

They are calling me; the shuttle is waiting. Now I must say good-bye to Thalassa forever. And your image, too, is beginning to fade. Though I am good at giving advice to others, perhaps I have clung too long to my own grief, and it does no service to your memory.

Thalassa has helped to cure me. Now I can rejoice that I knew you, rather than mourn because I lost you.

A strange calmness has come upon me. For the first time, I feel that I really understand my old Buddhist friends' concepts of Detachment—even of Nirvana . . .

And if I do not wake on Sagan Two, so be it. My work here is done, and I am well content.

55. DEPARTURE

The trimaran reached the edge of the kelp bed just before midnight, and Brant anchored in thirty meters of water. He would start to drop the spyballs at dawn, until the fence was laid between Scorpville and South Island. Once that was established, any comings and goings would be observed. If the scorps found one of the spyballs and carried it home as a trophy, so much the better. It would continue to operate, doubtless providing even more useful information than in the open sea.

Now there was nothing to do but to lie in the gently rocking boat and listen to the soft music from Radio Tarna, tonight uncharacteristically subdued. From time to time there would be an announcement or a message of goodwill or a poem in honor of the visitors. There could be few people sleeping on either island tonight; Mirissa wondered fleetingly what thoughts must be passing through the minds of Owen Fletcher and his fellow exiles, marooned on an alien world for the rest of their lives. The last time she had seen them on a Norther videocast, they had not appeared at all unhappy and had been cheerfully discussing local business opportunities.

Brant was so quiet that she would have thought he was sleeping except that his grip on her hand was as firm as ever as they lay side by side, looking up at the stars. He had changed—perhaps even more than she had. He was less impatient, more considerate. Best of all, he had already accepted the child, with words whose gentleness had reduced her to tears: "He will have two fathers."

Now Radio Tarna was starting the final and quite unnecessary launch countdown—the first that any Lassan had ever heard except for historic recordings from the past. Will we see anything at all, Mirissa wondered? *Magellan* is on the other side of the world, hovering at high noon above a hemisphere of ocean. We have the whole thickness of the planet between us . . .

". . . Z e r o . . ." Radio Tarna said—and instantly was obliterated by a roar of white noise. Brant reached for the gain control and had barely cut off the sound when the sky erupted.

The entire horizon was ringed with fire. North, south, east, west—there was no difference. Long streamers of flame reached up out of the ocean, halfway toward the zenith, in an auroral display such as Thalassa had never witnessed before, and would never see again.

It was beautiful but awe-inspiring. Now Mirissa understood why *Magellan* had been placed on the far side of the world; yet this was not the quantum drive itself but merely the stray energies leaking from it, being absorbed harmlessly in the ionosphere. Loren had told her something incomprehensible about superspace shockwaves, adding that not even the inventors of the drive had ever understood the phenomenon.

She wondered, briefly, what the scorps would make of these celestial fireworks; some trace of this actinic fury must surely filter down through the forests of kelp to illuminate the byways of their sunken cities.

Perhaps it was imagination, but the radiating, multicolored beams that formed the encircling crown of light seemed to be creeping slowly across the sky. The source of their energy was gaining speed, accelerating along its orbit as it left Thalassa forever. It was many minutes before she could be quite sure of the movement; in the same time, the intensity of the display had also diminished appreciably.

Then, abruptly, it ceased. Radio Tarna came back on the air, rather breathlessly.

". . . everything according to plan . . . the ship is now

being reorientated . . . other displays later, but not so spectacular . . . all stages of the initial breakaway will be on the other side of the world, but we'll be able to see *Magellan* directly in three days, when it's leaving the system . . ."

Mirissa scarcely heard the words as she stared up into the sky to which the stars were now returning—the stars that she could never see again without remembering Loren. She was drained of emotion now; if she had tears, they would come later.

She felt Brant's arms around her and welcomed their comfort against the loneliness of space. This was where she belonged; her heart would not stray again. For at last she understood; though she had loved Loren for his strength, she loved Brant for his weakness.

Good-bye, Loren, she whispered—may you be happy on that far world which you and your children will conquer for mankind. But think of me sometimes, three hundred years behind you on the road from Earth.

As Brant stroked her hair with clumsy gentleness, he wished he had words to comfort her, yet knew that silence was the best. He felt no sense of victory; though Mirissa was his once more, their old, carefree companionship was gone beyond recall. All the days of his life, Brant knew, the ghost of Loren would come between them—the ghost of a man who would not be one day older when they were dust upon the wind.

When, three days later, *Magellan* rose above the eastern horizon, it was a dazzling star too brilliant to look upon with the naked eye, even though the quantum drive had been carefully aligned so that most of its radiation leakage would miss Thalassa.

Week by week, month by month, it slowly faded, though even when it moved back into the daylight sky it was still easy to find if one knew exactly where to look. And at night, for years it was often the brightest of the stars.

245

Mirissa saw it one last time, just before her eyesight failed. For a few days the quantum drive—now harmlessly gentled by distance—must have been aimed directly toward Thalassa.

It was then fifteen light-years away, but her grandchildren had no difficulty in pointing out the blue, third magnitude star, shining above the watchtowers of the electrified scorp-barrier.

56. BELOW THE INTERFACE

They were not yet intelligent, but they possessed curiosity—and that was the first step along the endless road.

Like many of the crustaceans that had once flourished in the seas of Earth, they could survive on land for indefinite periods. Until the last few centuries, however, there had been little incentive to do so; the great kelp forests provided for all their needs. The long, slender leaves supplied food; the tough stalks were the raw material for their primitive artifacts.

They had only two natural enemies. One was a huge but very rare deep-sea fish—little more than a pair of ravening jaws attached to a never-satisfied stomach. The other was a poisonous, pulsing jelly—the motile form of the giant polyps—that sometimes carpeted the seabed with death, leaving a bleached desert in its wake.

Apart from sporadic excursions through the air–water interface, the scorps might well have spent their entire existence in the sea, perfectly adapted to their environment. But—unlike the ants and termites—they had not yet entered any of the blind alleys of evolution. They could still respond to change.

And change, although as yet only on a very small scale, had indeed come to this ocean world. Marvelous things had fallen out of the sky. Where these had come from, there must be more. When they were ready, the scorps would go in search of them.

There was no particular hurry in the timeless world of the Thalassan sea; it would be many years before they made their first assault upon the alien element from which their scouts had brought back such strange reports.

They could never guess that other scouts were reporting on *them*. And when they finally moved, their timing would be most unfortunate.

They would have the bad luck to emerge on land during President Owen Fletcher's quite unconstitutional but extremely competent second term of office.

IX. SAGAN TWO

57. THE VOICES OF TIME

The starship *Magellan* was still no more than a few light-hours distant when Kumar Lorenson was born, but his father was already sleeping and did not hear the news until three hundred years later.

He wept to think that his dreamless slumber had spanned the entire lifetime of his first child. When he could face the ordeal, he would summon the records that were waiting for him in the memory banks. He would watch his son grow to manhood and hear his voice calling across the centuries with greetings he could never answer.

And he would see (there was no way he could avoid it) the slow aging of the long-dead girl he had held in his arms—only weeks ago. Her last farewell would come to him from wrinkled lips long turned to dust.

His grief, though piercing, would slowly pass. The light of a new sun filled the sky ahead; and soon there would be another birth, on the world that was already drawing the starship *Magellan* into its final orbit.

One day the pain would be gone; but never the memory.

CHRONOLOGY (TERRAN YEARS)

1956	Detection of·neutrino		
1967	Solar neutrino anomaly discovered		
2000	Sun's fate confirmed		
100	Interstellar probes		
200			
300	Robot seeders planned		
400			
2500	Seeding started (embryos)		
600	(DNA codes)		
700			
	751 **Seeder Leaves for Thalassa**		
800			
900			
	999 **Last Millennium**		
3000		THALASSA	
100		3109 First Landing	0
200	**Lords**	Birth of Nation	100
	of	Contact with Earth	
300	**the**		200
	Last	Mt. Krakan Erupts,	
400	**Days**	Contact Lost	300
3500	**Quantum Drive**		400
600	**Final Exodus**	Stasis	
	617 **Starship** *Magellan*		
3620	**End of Earth**		
		3827 *Magellan* arrives	718
		3829 *Magellan* leaves	720
		4135 SAGAN TWO	1026

253

BIBLIOGRAPHICAL NOTE

The first version of this novel, a 12,500-word short story, was written between February and April 1957 and subsequently published in *IF* Magazine (US) for June 1958 and *Science Fantasy* (UK) in June 1959. It may be more conveniently located in my own Harcourt, Brace, Jovanovich collections *The Other Side of the Sky* (1958) and *From the Ocean, From the Stars* (1962).

In 1979, I developed the theme in a short movie outline that appeared in *OMNI Magazine* (Vol. 3, No. 12, 1980). This has since been published in the illustrated Byron Preiss/Berkley collection of my short stories *The Sentinel* (1984), together with an introduction explaining its origin and the unexpected manner in which it lead to the writing and filming of *2010: Odyssey Two*.

This novel, the third and final version, was begun in May 1983 and completed in June 1985.

July 1, 1985
Colombo, Sri Lanka

ACKNOWLEDGMENTS

The first suggestion that vacuum energies might be used for propulsion appears to have been made by Shinichi Seike in 1969. ("Quantum electric space vehicle"; 8th Symposium on Space Technology and Science, Tokyo)

Ten years later, H.D. Froning of McDonnell Douglas Astronautics introduced the idea at the British Interplanetary Societies' Interstellar Studies Conference, London (September 1969) and followed it up with two papers: "Propulsion Requirements for a Quantum Interstellar Ramjet" (*JBIS*, Vol. 33, 1980) and "Investigation of a quantum ramjet for interstellar flight" (*AIAA Preprint* 81-1534, 1981).

Ignoring the countless inventors of unspecified "space drives," the first person to use the idea in fiction appears to have been Dr. Charles Sheffield, chief scientist of Earth Satellite Corporation; he discusses the theoretical basis of the "quantum drive" (or, as he has named it, "vacuum energy drive") in his novel *The McAndrew Chronicles* (*Analog* magazine 1981; Tor, 1983).

An admittedly naive calculation by Richard Feynman suggests that every cubic centimeter of vacuum contains enough energy to boil all the oceans of Earth. Another estimate by John Wheeler gives a value a mere seventy-nine orders of magnitude *larger*. When two of the world's greatest physicists disagree by a little matter of seventy-nine zeroes, the rest of us may be excused a certain skepticism; but it's at least an interesting thought that the vacuum inside an ordinary light bulb contains enough energy to destroy the Galaxy . . . and perhaps, with a little extra effort, the Cosmos.

In what may hopefully be a historic paper ("Extracting electrical energy from the vacuum by cohesion of charged foliated conductors," *Physical Review*, Vol. 30B, pp. 1700–1702, August 15, 1984) Dr. Robert L. Forward of the Hughes Research Labs has shown that at least a minute fraction of this energy can be tapped. If it can be harnessed for propulsion by anyone besides science-fiction writers, the purely engineering problems of interstellar—or even intergalactic—flight would be solved.

But perhaps not. I am extremely grateful to Dr. Alan Bond for his detailed mathematical analysis of the shielding necessary for the mission described in this novel and for pointing out that a blunt cone is the most advantageous shape. It may well turn out that the factor limiting high-velocity interstellar flight will not be energy but ablation of the shield mass by dust grains, and evaporation by protons.

The history and theory of the "space elevator" will be found in my address to the Thirtieth Congress of the International Astronautical Federation, Munich, 1979: "The Space Elevator: 'Thought Experiment' or Key to the Universe?" (Reprinted in *Advances in Earth Orientated Applications of Space Technology*, Vol. I, No. 1, 1981, pp. 39–48 and *Ascent to Orbit*: John Wiley, 1984). I have also developed the idea in the novel *The Fountains of Paradise* (Del Rey, Gollancz, 1978).

The first experiments in this direction, involving payloads lowered into the atmosphere on hundred-kilometer-long "tethers" from the space shuttle, will be commencing around the time this novel is published.

My apologies to Jim Ballard and J.T. Frazer for stealing the title of their own two very different volumes for my final chapter.

My special gratitude to the Diyawadane Nilame and his staff at the Temple of the Tooth, Kandy, for kindly inviting me into the Relic Chamber during a time of troubles.

ABOUT THE AUTHOR

Arthur C. Clarke was born at Minehead, Somerset, England, in 1917 and is a graduate of Kings College, London, where he obtained First Class Honors in Physics and Mathematics. He is past Chairman of the British Interplanetary Society, a member of the Academy of Astronautics, the Royal Astronomical Society, and many other scientific organizations. During World War II, as an RAF officer, he was in charge of the first radar talk-down equipment during its experimental trials. His only *non*-science-fiction novel, *Glide Path*, is based on this work.

Author of fifty books, some twenty million-plus copies of which have been printed in over thirty languages, his numerous awards include the 1961 Kalinga Prize, the AAAS–Westinghouse science-writing prize, the Bradford Washburn Award, and the Hugo, Nebula, and John W. Campbell Awards—all three of which were won by his novel *Rendezvous with Rama*.

In 1968 he shared an Oscar nomination with Stanley Kubrick for *2001: A Space Odyssey*, and his thirteen-part TV series *Arthur C. Clarke's Mysterious World* has now been screened in many countries. He joined Walter Cronkite during CBS' coverage of the Apollo missions.

His invention of the communications satellite in 1945 has brought him numerous honors, such as the 1982 Marconi International Fellowship, a gold medal of the Franklin Institute, the Vikram Sarabhai Professorship of the Physical Research Laboratory, Ahmedabad, and a Fellowship of King's College, London. The President of Sri Lanka recently nominated him Chancellor of the University of Moratuwa, near Colombo.